Patricia Beatty

may 1981

RUFUS,
RED
RUFUS

Patricia Beatty

RUFUS, RED RUFUS

ILLUSTRATED BY TED LEWIN

William Morrow and Company
New York 1975

Copyright © 1975 by Patricia Beatty
All rights reserved. No part of this book may be reproduced or utilized
in any form or by any means, electronic or mechanical, including photo-
copying, recording or by any information storage and retrieval system,
without permission in writing from the Publisher. Inquiries should be
addressed to William Morrow and Company, Inc., 105 Madison Ave.,
New York, N.Y. 10016.
Printed in the United States of America.
1 2 3 4 5 79 78 77 76 75
Library of Congress Cataloging in Publication Data

Beatty, Patricia.
  Rufus, red Rufus.

  SUMMARY: Recounts the experiences of an Irish setter as he passes
from owner to owner on the campus of a California university.
  1. Dogs—Legends and stories. [1. Dogs—Fiction]
I. Lewin, Ted, ill. II. Title.
PZ10.3.B379Ru   [Fic]   74-26981
ISBN 0-688-22021-5
ISBN 0-688-32021-X lib. bdg.

CONTENTS

1
THEY'RE COMING, THEY'RE COMING

There were three of them tiptoeing down the hall. One was tall with black hair and wore ragged, cut-off jeans. One was short with blond hair and wore ragged, long jeans. The third young man had long brown hair and carried something in his arms. The something wriggled and squirmed, and once it let out a whimper.

"In there," whispered the black-haired college student. He pointed to the orange-painted door he'd stopped in front of. "This is Mad McCormick's room," he whispered.

"Are you sure he's in class now?" asked the student with long brown hair.

"Yeah, I saw him go in. He's in old Burns's class taking a test."

"Yeech, English history! That course wrecks a lot of B averages. Old Burns sure likes to give low grades." The blond student snorted at the very thought of Professor Burns. He opened the orange door cautiously, stuck his shaggy head inside, and then beckoned. "Come on. It's okay. Hey, McCormick's bed's even made! That proves he's crazy. Dump it on top of the bed."

"Okay." The brown-haired student went into the room. He put what he had in his arms down onto the blue bedspread. It was a puppy, a puppy the color of an old copper penny but sleek and shining the way old pennies never are.

"You stay here, dog," he told the puppy. And out he went into the hall, hurrying down its long polished length with the others to the stairway.

Alone! The little Irish setter let out a snuffling sound as he waddled across the bedspread. He looked over the edge of the bed gauging the distance to the floor. It was a long way down. Deciding against jumping off, he walked back to the center of the bed, made four complete circles on its top, and finally collapsed. It wasn't the easiest thing in the world to collapse— not with a long, stiff greeting card tied to his puppy flea collar. The card, which wasn't at all comfortable, kept sticking into his jaw.

*   *   *

David McCormick came frowning into his dormitory room an hour later. The examination on the history of England had been a real brute. He could put all he knew about some of the kings of England into one eye and not even make it bloodshot. William Rufus had come to the throne of England after his father, who was William the Conqueror, had died. David knew something about William the Conqueror. After all he had conquered England! But he didn't know anything much about old King William Rufus. He knew only that William Rufus had had red hair and a foul temper. He was called Rufus because his hair was red, and in Latin *rufus* meant *red*.

McCormick talked to himself a great deal. Sometimes he even answered himself. It didn't bother him because he thought he was good company. But it bothered a lot of other people on this campus of the University of California. Watching him wander about muttering to himself got on their nerves.

Now, still holding his notebooks under his arm, he scratched his head while he scowled. He said very slowly and very clearly to himself, "Old man Burns is out to get me. He's gonna give me a D in this test I took today. I just know it. And if he gives me a D, that could be the end of my B average here." The student moaned. "And if I don't get a B average in all of the subjects I'm taking, I won't get into medical school and I won't even get to be a doctor." He paused. "And if I know I'm going to get a D at the end of this year, I'll do something nobody around here will ever forget. And then I'll head for home. You bet I will!"

Flinging his notebooks onto his desk, McCormick was about to throw himself down onto the bed and kick at the wall. Just in time he noticed the red puppy. He caught himself in mid-flop only a few feet from the top of the bed. "Hey—what the . . .?" he cried out. He picked the puppy up, awakening him, and reached for the card around his neck. Twisting the dog and the card so he could see, David McCormick read aloud:

October 15, Tuesday

All Irish setters are supposed to be nuts.
All Irishmen who climb bell towers
   when the regents are here are nuts.
All redheads are nuts.
This dog is red and nuts.
Your hair just matches his.
   Ashes to ashes,
   Dust to dust,
   Nuts to nuts.

With our compliments,
   your anonymous friends and admirers

P.S. The dog was born in Lothian Hall in a clothes closet during summer session. He is a he. We guarantee this.

"Oh, Lord," exploded McCormick. He looked at himself and the dog in his mirror. He guessed who his anonymous friends were—junior students like himself but living in another dormitory on campus. What they had written was sort of true. He and the dog did look alike. His hair was the color of the setter's. McCormick peered into the animal's sleepy face. It opened dark brown eyes, closed them, then opened its pink mouth in a huge yawn. McCormick bent nearer to the mirror. His eyes really were "puppy-dog brown." What the pretty girl living on the other floor of his dormitory had told him was true. He had "large, soulful, puppy-dog-brown eyes—brown velvet eyes." He sighed deeply and stuck out his tongue at his reflection. It was pink too.

He put the setter back onto his bed and sat down beside it, watching it curl into a russet satin ball and fall asleep. He began to mutter again, "Well, it seems I've got a pooch. Well, why not? Everybody else here's got a dog. It's the thing to do these days." He laughed and patted the puppy. "You're Irish, too, huh? Two Irishmen ought to stick together. What's your name? They didn't put that on the card."

The puppy snuffled in his sleep.

"Snuffles? No, not that. I wouldn't call any dog that." McCormick pondered a name, and as he did he gazed around his bare little room. All at once he said, "Billy the Kid?" He shook his head. He thought some more, then came out with, "William Burns? No, I couldn't do that to a dog either." All at once he snapped his big fingers. "How about William Rufus? King William. No, that's not right. But Rufus is! Just Rufus. Hey, dog, did you know that Rufus means *red*?"

McCormick stroked the puppy's spine as he went on. "You know, it'll be nice to have somebody to talk to besides myself when I'm in here." He chuckled. "Though some people who say I'm nuts won't think talking to a dog's so good either. I hope you're a little bit nuts, old Rufus, the way Irish setters are supposed to be. You'll have to be a little bit crazy to keep up with my reputation. Sometimes I do crazy things. That's because studying all the time gets to me, and I break loose." A dreamy smile spread over the young man's face. "Boy, do I ever bust loose!"

He tickled Rufus under the jaw next. "I have friends here who have to break loose, too—especially in the springtime. By then we've taken too many tests and read too many books. We got to bust loose or we got to quit school."

He lifted Rufus up. Holding the puppy, he lay down full-length on his bed and set Rufus onto his chest where he could stare into the dog's face. He said softly while Rufus lay sleepily on him, "You know, you're lucky to be a dog. You don't have to worry about keeping your grades high so you can hang onto your scholarship, and you don't have to worry about money. There aren't any pockets in a dog collar. Do you like pizza, Rufus? You'd better like it because that's what I mostly live on. I've got a night job at a pizza parlor. I'll bring pizza home with me, and I'll do something more, too. I'll introduce you to my old buddy, Señora Perez."

And so McCormick did—the very next day.

Because of Señora Perez Rufus in time became a

fine, strong dog with a coat that burned copper-bright in the sunlight as he raced across the campus lawns trying to leap up and catch mockingbirds that dived at the top of his head to peck him. Rufus hated only two things in the world—mockingbirds, those loud, scolding gray-and-white flying things that he could never catch, and the campus cats.

He liked all of the people he met. But he loved only two of them—David McCormick and Señora Perez.

Both of them fed him.

Señora Perez was a short, plump woman, who worked in the kitchen of the dormitory McCormick lived in. She was a Mexican-American woman whose husband had died and whose children had grown up and gone away. She pitied the poor ragged-looking college students—particularly the young men. If she thought one of them looked thin or pale when he came up to her in the cafeteria line, she'd put an extra spoonful of potatoes and gravy onto his plate and push the biggest piece of pie forward for him to take. She had had three sons who were always hungry and who never had any money either.

Señora Perez had a very fond spot for David Mc-Cormick, who was very poor, very thin, and always worried about his grades. He reminded her of her second son, who had worried about school and tests he had to take. Her son had gotten A's and B's, but he always expected something worse. He had had a scholarship also. Her son had told her all his troubles just the way David McCormick did. She had enjoyed worrying with her son, and now that he was out of school and a successful businessman, a supermarket manager, she missed his troubles.

Her first sight of Rufus occurred when McCormick came after lunch to the back door of the kitchen and called out her name. She went out, looking curious, wiping her hands on her apron. And then she spied the red puppy in his arms.

"Davido, what have you got there?" she asked.

"My dog," he replied. Then he asked, "Have you got a handful of milk anywhere around you, señora?"

She giggled at that. Her son was quite humorous, too. She went back inside and appeared with a bowl and a little paper carton. "Davido, are you permitted to keep dogs?" she wanted to know, as she poured out the milk for Rufus.

"No, but everybody and his dog's got a dog here at this college. How about you? Have you got a dog?"

Señora Perez shook her head, making her long golden earrings sway. "No, I have such a tiny apartment. The manager does not permit even a cat." She smiled. "I have a goldfish. One goldfish only. It is not much company for me." She looked sad.

"Señora?" McCormick shifted his large feet. "Do you suppose you could save some meat scraps for my dog sometimes?"

She gazed at the puppy out of mournful dark eyes. "Yes, I think I could."

The student let out his breath. "Hey, that'll be great. Can you put them somewhere where I can get them?"

She nodded. "*Sí*, on top of the back wall in a paper bag. Look for a paper bag when you go by here in the afternoons, and please do not tell other students or my lady boss about it."

He asked, "Señora, could giving Rufus scraps cost you your job?"

"No, not if they are only leftover scraps, but still it is best not to tell that I am doing it."

"Okay." McCormick picked up Rufus, who had drunk only a little milk, from the grass. He said, "Rufus thanks you, and I thank you."

"Davido," the woman asked, "what are you planning to do next? What bad thing will you do now?"

"Huh? Nothing. What do you mean, señora?"

She reached out as if to pat Rufus, but her hand fastened onto McCormick's skinny arm. "There is much talk about you here. It is said that last spring you brought a horse, a large gray horse, into the dining room of the Faculty Club just before a banquet."

"Yeah, I did. Do you think it was easy getting the horse?" He smiled at the happy memory.

"Ah, but, Davido, the week after that you painted green footprints up the walls of the library. You might have fallen and killed yourself."

"Oh, no, señora." The young man shook his head violently. "Some of my friends hauled me and the paint and brush up on ropes. They're football players. *Mucho* muscle, you know."

"Davido," she said softly, "I saw the smoke in the sky two weeks ago."

He smiled once more as he fondled Rufus's ears.

"Yeah, wasn't that good? It was one of my very best. I've got a friend here who used to be in the Air Force. He has his own plane in town, or rather his old man does, and we borrowed it. This guy and I are both in Professor Burns's history class. That's why he did the skywriting for us. Didn't the smoke come out loud and clear?"

She sighed. "I remember it well, Davido. My neck is still stiff from trying to read it. It said: *Venita. Marry me at once. Willy Burns.*"

Señora Perez's voice changed. "Dr. Burns is Willy Burns. He is a married man. Venita is dean of women, and she has never married." She released David's arm. "The dean of women will not like you for that nor will Professor Burns. Davido, you will go too far one day soon. I fear for you." She fixed him with a look of deep concern. How pleasant it was to worry over somebody again. "And day before yesterday what did you do? You climbed the bell tower without a rope. And the regents were here watching you. People called out to you from below to come down, but you would not. Why did you do such a wild and crazy thing?"

McCormick scowled. "I did it because the regents were here. I was protesting their coming again. There were twelve regents watching me and three deans yelling for me to get down. I ignored all fifteen of them and went all the way to the top."

"*Ay de mí*, Davido, you will be killed or you will be expelled. They will kick you out of this school."

He laughed. "I've been told that by two deans, three professors, and my best girl already."

"Oh, Davido."

McCormick shook his head so violently that it alarmed Rufus, who snorted. "When I have to bust loose because too many people are pushing me, I bust loose. It's the Irish in me, I guess. If I didn't do those things now and then, I'd explode." He ruffled the puppy's bright fur. "The pressure gets real bad on students around here in the spring of the year."

"But, Davido, this is autumn, and already you have done two bad things."

He sighed. "It's starting with me early this year. That's because of old Professor Burns. He works everybody in his class like an animal. I think he hates students."

"Poor unhappy man," came from Señora Perez.

"Poor man—hah! Yeah, in his class a student leads a dog's life. I just hope I can get a B out of him." He stooped and picked up the milk bowl and handed it to her. "I wonder what kind of a dog Rufus will be by the time spring rolls around?" he remarked.

"I wonder, too," Señora Perez echoed, as McCormick walked off carrying the red puppy and the carton of milk.

In several months' time everyone on the campus knew the answer to Mad McCormick's question because nearly everyone knew Rufus McCormick! Rufus intercepted Frisbees and ran off with them in his mouth, and he was absolutely the worst bicycle chaser the school had ever known. No one was safe from him. He chased students and professors alike, running beside them biting at the bottoms of their trousers. He chewed up cotton and wool and polyester and once even the pink lace of a coed's pantsuit. Bicycle riders swatted him with notebooks and rolled-up newspapers. Twice people tried to bash him with books taken out of their baskets, a history of France and a collection of Shakespeare's plays. Rufus dodged both of them skillfully as he ran after their bicycles.

"Mad McCormick's mad mutt," some of the professors called him.

Running free with never a leash on him, scuffling with other college dogs, sometimes winning the fights, and chasing cats around the greenhouses, Rufus became a very well-known member of the college community.

One hot spring day, however, his life of joy came to an end. That day he and McCormick were lolling under a tree in front of the dormitory. His head pillowed on a sleeping Rufus's flank, McCormick looked up and saw Señora Perez coming toward him. She had taken her apron off. Being polite to ladies, McCormick got up and pointed to Rufus, who went right on sleeping. "People talk about how hard it is to lead a dog's life, señora," he said. "Just look at old Rufus there. Not a care in the world. He's being fed in two places and is bulking up more every day. He's a fine broth of a dog and the king of the campus."

Señora Perez looked more mournful than usual. "Davido, there is something that I must tell you. Your dog may be king of the campus today. But what of tomorrow? What of *mañana*?"

McCormick laughed. "What do you mean about tomorrow? Rufus has his health and two places to eat, and I've kept my job at the pizza parlor."

She didn't laugh with him. She said quietly, "Davido, the regents are coming. They come. They come soon."

"Oh God, *again*? They were here twice last year and already once this year!" David let out a groan that made Rufus wake up. The dog rose to his feet and looked up into the sky. McCormick told Señora Perez, "Rufus is looking out for mockingbirds. When I groaned, I suppose he thought one of them was pecking me. He has a thing about mockingbirds. Hey, señora, are you sure about the regents?"

Señora Perez smiled as Rufus came to rub against her and be patted. "I heard some of the college secretaries talking while they went through the cafeteria lines. They ate lunch here today as guests of some of the girl students. Davido, the secretaries are always right. They know everything."

McCormick smacked his hand to his forehead. "I know. I know. So the regents are coming! I remember when they were here last fall. That's when I climbed the bell tower with a sign on my back saying *Regents Go Home*!" Staring at Rufus, who had slumped down near Señora Perez's foot, McCormick wanted to know, "When are the regents due?"

"Next week, Davido. They will stay a couple of days—as they always do. *Ay de mí*, the regents are such terrible trouble! The cleaning and the polishing we must do in the kitchen! You can see your face in the tile floor when the regents walk through inspecting."

"Next week." McCormick moaned this time. He asked, "Señora, when will the big dog roundup begin?"

"Very soon. Any day now, I think."

"Yeah, that's what I think, too. Rufus," David told the setter, "you have to leave then. If I don't get you out of here, you'll be rounded up by the campus police and hauled off to the dog pound in town. I didn't get you until last October. The regents were here the month before. I suppose somebody else saved you from them by hiding you in a clothes closet when they went through the dormitories. But you're too big now to be hidden away in my clothes closet."

"Davido, board him with the animal doctor on University Avenue."

McCormick hooted. Rufus came away from Señora Perez's shoes. He'd been sniffing them, smelling the lemon-scented floor wax on them. A hooting sound like that was sometimes the signal for a tussle on the grass with his master. But not this time. Instead, McCormick took him by the green plastic collar Señora Perez had given Rufus for Christmas and spoke to her. "Look, he's got the collar you got for him, but he hasn't got a dog license yet. I can't afford to buy one for him until I get some cash ahead, and I sure can't bail him out at the dog pound if the campus police pick him up as a stray. It's all I can do to keep him in cold pizza, and I couldn't afford to keep him at all if you didn't feed him, too." He looked somberly at Rufus. "Poor dog. No regent must ever have to look at a dog running free. There must be no dogs seen sniffing at a shrub or a tree because the sight might shock a regent. Dogs have been known to make messes. And a very long-legged regent on another campus was once said to have been mistaken for a tree by a nearsighted dog. What am I going to do with you, Rufus, me darling, while the regents are here?"

Rufus lifted his front right paw, one of the two tricks he'd learned from David. The word *darling* was a signal for it. McCormick took the paw and sadly shook it. "Rufus," he went on, holding the paw, "you are young and innocent. You do not know what the regents are. They are gods. They wear four-hundred-dollar suits spun out of cobwebs and moonbeams. They wear two-hundred-dollar shoes, though their feet never touch dirt or grass. They walk only on carpets. They eat steak off plates of solid gold. A regent never looks through a dusty window on a campus. When they come around inspecting this campus, *everything* gets washed and polished. The buildings, the windows, the campus cars—the staff, the professors."

Señora Perez giggled in spite of herself. "Not the students, Davido, but all else you say is truth."

David McCormick sighed. "No, not the students.

Though there isn't a student here who doesn't know
that when the regents come the students must behave
like ladies and gentlemen. Dog"—David put his red
head next to the dog's red one after he'd released the
paw he'd been shaking—"the governor of the State
of California sometimes comes with the regents. He
is a regent. He runs the state and the regents run the
University of California." He lifted the setter's head
in his big freckled hand. "Even if you were born in a
clothes closet here and have always spent your days on
the campus, while those holy beings, the regents, are
here you must hide out. Me darling, you have to get
off the campus!" Again Rufus raised his paw, and
David took it to shake.

Then he asked Señora Perez over Rufus's head,
"Does anybody friendly that you know live off campus, señora? I haven't got a car so it can't be very far
away from here. I'll have to walk Rufus over."

"*Sí*." She nodded. "Mr. Revengo, Eustace Revengo.
Everybody knows him. He is the man from Africa
who gives lectures about Africa. The graduate student who wears the very strange shirts."

"Sure. I know him. How did you know him? He
lives in Canyon Crest."

"Avocados," she said calmly. "He came to see me
to ask me how we Mexicans fix avocados. He is interested in them."

McCormick looked doubtfully at Rufus. "What
if the regents decide they want to inspect Canyon
Crest student housing, where the married graduate

students live? There aren't supposed to be any pets there either."

Señora Perez told McCormick while Rufus ran off chasing a low-flying yellow butterfly, "Mr. Revengo is a good man. He would take your dog next week, I am certain. I could keep watch for the regents, and if I heard anyone saying that they were going to Canyon Crest, I could call Mr. Revengo on the telephone for you and warn him. He could move the dog in time."

"Yeah, it could work," mused McCormick. "If they were on their way there and Revengo got warned in time, he could take Rufus across Blaine Street. Over Blaine he's off the campus and out of the regents' territory. It's a whole new world out there over Blaine." He gestured toward the northern mountains.

"Davido, do you know anyone who lives on Blaine so you could take Rufus there now?"

He let out a loud snort. "The only one I know is Professor Burns!"

"*Him?*" Señora Perez looked alarmed. "How do you know where he lives? You say that you hate him, that poor man."

"I hate him with a white-hot passion. He's aiming to give me a D at the end of this quarter. I know it. He's reading a test paper of mine right now, and I know that's going to be a D, too. I checked out Burns's address because I wanted to put firecrackers in his mailbox on Saint Patrick's Day. I didn't do it, though. I couldn't buy any. Besides I hear that old Burns has kids. I don't want to scare them. It must be hard enough for them having an old man like that without having firecrackers exploding in their mailbox. Professors!"

"Oh, Davido, some professors are very nice men."

He let out a sorrowful sound. "Burns is not nice. He is a cat man. He's very antidog. He brags about being a cat man. He even keeps a picture of his cats in his office. He doesn't like dogs in the lecture hall. Rufus sat down in front of Burns once last January and stared at him for fifty minutes while he lectured to us. Rufus didn't let out a sound, but it sure rattled Burns all right. He knows Rufus is my dog because after the lecture Rufus came up to me and walked out with me. You should have seen the mean look Burns gave us."

"Poor man," breathed Señora Perez. "Davido, shall I call Mr. Revengo for you?"

2
ACROSS BLAINE

One night several days later Rufus had a bath in the dormitory showers along with McCormick and later was brushed to an auburn brilliance. Then on a leash of braided rope, he walked with his master to the Canyon Crest Housing Development. According to Señora Perez, who was listening very carefully to rumors passed up and down the cafeteria line at lunch, the dog roundup began the next morning, and the regents were due the day after. She had arranged with Mr. Revengo that he take Rufus for a time.

The setter didn't like the leash. He got wound up in it and tripped over it. David McCormick didn't like it either, because he also got wound up in it and tripped over it. They were both a little bit out of sorts when they reached Revengo's house. It was really only half a house. The other half had green shutters; Revengo's had brown ones. Both halves were occupied by married graduate students with children.

Mrs. Revengo opened the door to David's knock. She was tall and dark and wearing a long patterned dress of brown, black, and bright yellow. There was a yellow turban over her hair.

"Well, here we are, ma'am," said McCormick. "I've kept Rufus as long as I could, and now it's time for him to come here. He's been out of sight in the dorms or in parked cars in case the campus police started to spring a surprise dog hunt. They'll really get busy tomorrow, I hear tell."

Instead of nodding, the woman smiled. Then she shook her head and put her finger to her lips. The three small Revengo children didn't even smile. There they stood, two girls and a boy, behind their mother, staring through the screen door at the red dog and the red-haired young man.

Rufus, who seldom saw children, stared at them in return. They were very small to be human beings. Children rarely came onto the campus.

Mrs. Revengo went away without asking Mc-Cormick and the setter inside the house. They could hear her voice calling inside, though, but not in words David could understand. Now he knew why she'd put her finger to her lips. She had not been telling him to speak softly but that she didn't know the English language. "That's it. She can't talk English," McCormick told Rufus. "But don't you worry. Mr. Revengo does. He talks it better than I do. He's gone to school in England. Now he's come to California to study all about avocados so he can go back to Africa and grow them there." He sighed, stooped, and patted Rufus. "I'll drop off some pizza every night on my way home from work. I don't know what you'll be eating here, but I don't think it'll be pizza."

Mr. Revengo was a very large black man in a pale green, loose-fitting, much-embroidered *dashiki*—the "very strange shirt" that Señora Perez had mentioned. Mr. Revengo always wore *dashikis* his wife had made and embroidered for him. He shook hands with David out on the porch, then stood teetering back and forth on his heels and toes looking down at Rufus. He asked in a soft deep voice with an English accent, "What does the animal eat?"

"Pizza mostly."

"Pizza?" Revengo's voice rose to a squeak of astonishment.

"Oh, he eats most anything really, but he likes pizza. It makes people on campus complain that he's got a garlic breath, but that doesn't bother Rufus and me."

Revengo smiled. He knew David McCormick by reputation and by sight, and he had been impressed when the young man had climbed the bell tower. He had also been delighted with the skywriting. Revengo

had taken his wife and children out into their backyard to look up into the sky, and he had spelled out
the words letter by letter for them.

Now he asked David a question that floored the
student.

"Does he eat ground nuts, for instance?"

"What are ground nuts?"

Mr. Revengo chuckled. "I am referring to what
you Americans call peanuts. Does your dog eat peanut butter?"

Rufus heard David's sigh of relief. "Rufus dotes on
peanut butter. He likes jelly, too."

"Excellent, excellent." Revengo beamed. "We eat
a lot of ground-nut butter here." He took the leash
from David and hauled Rufus into the front room.
It was a very small bare room with a grass rug on the
floor. By the time Rufus had crossed the room, the
rug was piled up against the opposite wall.

"It's only temporary," McCormick called from the
doorway to the man and the dog.

"Yes, yes," agreed a panting Revengo, as the door
and screen door were closed by McCormick. "When
the regents go home, you go home!" Revengo told the
dog. Rufus with him, Mr. Revengo went out through
the kitchen. Claws scraping on the linoleum, Rufus
was hauled out into the fenced backyard. And there
he was tethered to a clothesline pole.

Alone! He was *alone*! Rufus let out howl after
heartbroken howl as darkness came down upon him.
Where was David McCormick? Why was he tied up?

Why did no one come to him? And why were the drums from inside the house so loud they hurt his ears?

At his family's bedtime hour, Mr. Revengo stopped practicing on his little drums for the African music concert he was giving at the end of the month. He came out at last to bring the red dog a plastic bowl of water. He spoke to Rufus, who had stopped his howling the moment Revengo had finished the drumming and come outside. "Ah, dog, you have the true spirit of the wild Irish. Never content. Howl away. Vent your sorrow. Be our banshee."

When Rufus bent to drink, because howling was thirsty work, Revengo patted him and told him, "Not to worry. We will keep you safe from the regents and the campus police. The police will not come here to snare dogs unless they know the regents are visiting Canyon Crest. The police are aware of our dogs and cats and other pets. They pretend not to notice that we have them.

"But if the regents do come, I will take you away in good time. I will be warned by the nice Mexican lady who works in the dormitory cafeteria and who knows so much about the uses of avocados. She will call me in my home so I will be warned. Try to be happy, dog. Perhaps my children will even play with you in time."

Revengo laughed softly and deeply again. "Our baby-sitter lives across Blaine Street. If the worst comes to the worst and the regents inspect here, too,

I will ask Sandy Burns to take you home with her. She would take very good care of you across Blaine Street. Such a nice girl! From such a nice family! So friendly!"

Rufus didn't get along very well with any of the Revengos except for Mr. Revengo. First of all, Mrs. Revengo seemed to be afraid of him. She hung her laundry down by the opposite clothespole, where Rufus couldn't reach her. When he barked at her, wanting some attention, she jumped straight up into the air dropping the clothespin out of her mouth. She didn't feed him either, though using the garden hose she kept the water in his bowl fresh. She was very careful about that—careful to squirt the water at the bowl, not at the dog. Rufus had hoped to be squirted. He liked it. David and the other students had often squirted him with hoses. So had the gardeners working on the campus. They knew that there was nothing the setter liked better than to lie down in the ivy in front of a campus building on a hot day when the sprinkling system was going. Squirting was second-best to having the sprinklers spouting all around him, but it was better than nothing to a water-loving dog.

Two of the Revengo children kept far away from Rufus, too, though they sat for hours the next two days, Wednesday and Thursday, on the back steps watching him. Rufus watched them, too. But they didn't throw Frisbees or balls for him to run after. They didn't even speak to him or call out his name or feed him, though one of them sang to herself sometimes in a high, thin voice. Because they were there and because she was singing and he could hear and see somebody, Rufus didn't howl.

The third Revengo, the smallest girl, was bolder than her brother and sister. All day Thursday while the newly arrived regents were inspecting the school, going from building to building, she sat staring at Rufus out of round black eyes. She didn't sit on the steps with the other two. Not she, not this Revengo. She sat on the grass near a clump of red canna lilies. The next morning, Friday, she tottered straight up to Rufus, who ran to the end of his leash to greet her. She put her arms around his neck and laid her cheek against his muzzle. Rufus drew back to lick his tongue across her face. She'd very recently had a peanut-butter sandwich.

And then she did something no one had ever done to him before. She flung a leg over his back and, pulling on his ears, hauled herself aboard him. From there, astride him, she said one word, "Horsie."

Rufus didn't snap at her or growl or even snarl. Shocked, he simply collapsed. And then he howled. He howled again and again.

All three of the Revengo children howled, too! And their mother came rushing out the back door. She shrieked, "Deena!"

This was the name of the smallest child. Hearing it made her look up from her place atop Rufus. A few more words from her mother got her up off the Irish setter. A pointing finger and a torrent of words forced her to leave the dog and run sobbing to her mother. Mrs. Revengo picked her daughter up, shooed the other two inside the house, and slammed the back door.

She left Rufus on his belly on the grass next to his water dish, too amazed at what had just happened to let out a single sound. He didn't see another Revengo all that day, but that night Mr. Revengo came out to him with a cold pizza David had brought over and left on the front porch on his way back to the dormitories from work the night before. It had been in the refrigerator all day long and was ice-cold.

"I put ground-nut butter on it for you," said the man.

Rufus accepted it, cold as it was, for he had yet to taste hot pizza. He wolfed it down as fast as Mr. Revengo could tear it apart for him.

And then the African spoke to Rufus. "Dog, we have a problem that must be sorted out tonight. There have been some new events on the campus. The regents have walked through the dormitories checking to see if the beds were made, and they have looked at the condition of the blackboards and the lighting in the classroom buildings. The word I have received from the Mexican lady who knows about avocados is that they are coming next to Canyon Crest. The nice woman called me from the cafeteria today. Tomorrow morning the mighty regents are visiting the graduate-student housing—and that means *us*. Although tomorrow is a Saturday, they are coming. And the governor of the State of California is coming. All cats and dogs hereabouts are disappearing tonight."

Revengo put his hands on his hips. "Now, if you were only a forbidden cat, we could hide you under the bed in a box. But you are so large that my small Deena thinks you are a red horse. You must cross Blaine Street, and you must cross tonight. Sandy Burns is baby-sitting for us this evening. When I drive her home, you will go with her. It is all arranged. I have told her." And the man threw Rufus, who had been waiting, the last piece of pizza.

Rufus stared after Revengo, whose yellow *dashiki* was a pale blur as he walked away and went into the house. Then he ate the pizza. Then he started to howl.

Hours went by until the back door opened once more. Lying with his head on his paws, exhausted from howling, Rufus was awakened by its clicking sound. He got up. More food? He licked his chops, savoring the traces of peanut butter. He had never had peanut butter on pizza before, but it wasn't a combination to be turned down.

This time it wasn't Mr. Revengo, who smelled of kitchen spices. Rufus's nose told him that and also that it wasn't McCormick, who often smelled of garlic and onions because of his pizza making. No! The setter wrinkled his nose. This person smelled of vanilla—like ice cream. Rufus was very partial to ice-cream cones as long as somebody held them for him to lick.

Sandra Burns came slowly forward toward the red dog, who she saw was lying, head on his paws, in the moonlight. The Revengo children were all asleep, and she'd agreed to take the dog till Sunday when the regents were definitely to be off the campus until next year. She knew just how she was going to arrange it.

While the Revengo children got ready for bed, fifteen-year-old Sandy had called her younger sister Charmian at home.

"Char," she'd said over the phone, "the Revengos have got a problem."

Thirteen-year-old Charmian had sniffed into the receiver. "Who hasn't got a problem? Won't any avocados grow for poor Mr. Revengo? All he has to do is get a seed, stick some toothpicks in it, put it in a glass of water, take it back to Africa, stick it in the ground, and. . . ."

"No, no, no," Sandy had told her. "It hasn't got anything to do with avocados. It's about Rufus McCormick."

"Huh?" Then there was a giggle. "What'll Eric say to that?"

"Char," Sandy had explained, trying to keep her temper, "Rufus is not a boy. Rufus is a dog."

"Dog? Did you say *d-o-g*?"

"Congratulations. You can spell! The problem is that the dog's got to get off the campus tonight. Pronto."

"What did he do? Bite somebody important?" Charmian sounded more thoughtful at last.

"No, it's the regents. They aren't supposed to see dogs."

"Oh, them?" There was silence. "Yeah, Dad said they were here most of the week—a lot longer than people expected them to stay. I bet that's why both of his socks matched every day he's gone over to the campus."

"Probably. I noticed that, too. Well, Mr. Revengo has asked us to hide Rufus."

The reply was one flat word. "Where?"

"*Unter das Haus.* You know what that means. When Mr. Revengo takes me home, I'll bring the dog."

Sandy heard her sister's deep sigh. "Can't you sneak him back onto the campus tonight—back to whoever it is who owns him. It isn't very nice *unter das Haus.*"

"No. It's McCormick, Mad McCormick, who owns him."

"Oh, no!" came a soft wail from Charmian. "We've heard of him! He doesn't like Dad one little bit."

Sandy hurried on. "Mr. Revengo tried to call the pizza parlor where McCormick works tonight, but the boy who answered the phone said McCormick wasn't there. He doesn't know where he is. Besides we can't go onto the campus now. Mr. Revengo says the campus police are still out after dogs. They cornered a Labrador retriever in one of the greenhouses this morning. He and the police broke an awful lot of flower pots before he was grabbed and put into the Humane Society truck."

"Hmmn." That convinced Charmian. "Well, okay. What do you want me to do, Sandy?"

"Get it ready *unter das Haus.* You know, a pan of water and some food."

"What flavor?" Charmian laughed. "We've got sardines and fresh ocean fish and mackerel and tuna fish."

"Make it meat. Our cats have plenty of kidney and liver and chicken flavors. Use one of those."

"Sure. It'll be ready when you come home. Just tell the dog not to let out one little bark or he's in big trouble and so are we."

"I'll tell him. Good-bye."

So now Sandra approached Rufus, speaking softly to him with her clenched fist stretched out in front of her for him to sniff. He came to the length of his leash and snuffled at it. Yes, vanilla ice cream. He smelled her shoes and trousers, too. They didn't smell quite so nice. In fact, they smelled of cats. There were lots of cats on the campus. The hair on Rufus's spine bristled.

"Rufus," the girl told him in a soft voice, "you'll be going home with me tonight. On Sunday afternoon I'll walk you back to the campus and try to find Mad McCormick. I guess everybody there knows who he is. I won't tell him who my dad is, though." She made a small sound that might have been a sigh. "I sure hope two things—number one, that Dad doesn't see you, and number two, that if he does, he doesn't recognize whose dog you are. I doubt if he'd have a McCormick anything around—even *unter das Haus.*" Then she heaved a bigger sigh, a definite one. "And you've got to beware of the cats. Remember, you're just a guest. They live with Dad."

At ten forty-five Mr. Revengo came out to untie Rufus. The setter let out a yelp of joy and went bounding ahead of Revengo through the side gate of the chain link fence. He jerked the African along to the old Ford parked out in the street. To Rufus, one of the high spots in life was a ride in a car. Any car. Anybody's car. Cars went swiftly. Wonderful new odors flowed one after another to a dog's nose as a dog stood on the seat with his head out the open window. Wind rushing past blew a dog's ears about in delightful confusion. And then there was the sheer happiness of turning around to slather a tongue over someone's face. A face was always at just the right level in a car.

Revengo opened the back door. Like a flash Rufus was inside and clawing his way over onto the front seat where Sandy was sitting.

"Hey," she said. "He looks as if he wants to go."

"He does indeed." Mr. Revengo sounded happy. He felt guilty because he hadn't been able to make McCormick's dog a part of his family even for a little while. But his wife, who knew so very little English, was afraid that the setter wouldn't obey her commands. Revengo also knew that the campus dogs had had very little contact with small children. Who knows what might have happened if one of his had pulled the dog's tail hard or put a hand into his mouth to see how sharp his teeth were?

As he started the car and drove off, he told himself, "Perhaps the dog takes after David McCormick in truth. There is absolutely no predicting what that young man will do. I couldn't get him on the phone at the pizza parlor tonight, and no one there seemed to know anything about his whereabouts." He turned to Sandy, peering past Rufus, who was sitting on the seat staring out through the windshield. "Do you happen to know David McCormick?"

"No." She was twisting a strand of her blond hair around a finger. "But I've sure heard of him. Isn't he the one who stuck a sign *Unfair to All Students* on the door of my dad's office last fall?"

"Ah, I knew such a sign had been put on a professor's door by McCormick, but I didn't know it was put on your father's."

"Well, it was. He signed it. He must have been crazy to sign it. Dad hates him."

Mr. Revengo nodded as they made a right turn out of the housing development. "Last month McCormick came in the back door of the hall where your father was lecturing. McCormick was wearing long woolen underwear and was on a skateboard. He went down the side of the lecture hall and out the front door waving a checkered red-and-white flag. People have claimed the young man is around the bend."

"What does that mean?"

"Mad as a March hare."

"Oh, Alice and the rabbit and the wonderland, huh?"

"Exactly."

"What about the dog? Is he around the bend too?"

Revengo cleared his throat. "Irish setters are rather nervy dogs, I've heard."

"What does that mean? Will he steal a steak off the stove?"

"No, no, it simply means what you call nervous."

"Are you sure it doesn't mean nuts?" Sandy asked doubtfully, as she held tight to Rufus's collar to keep him from sitting down on Mr. Revengo and interfering with his driving. Revengo's English slang sometimes confused her.

Revengo said, "No, but he does like ground-nut butter." This time the man translated. "I refer to peanut butter. He might be a bit odd. Irish setters can be sometimes a little mental, you know."

"Yes, I think I know what you mean now."

"Where will you keep him, Sandy?"

"Out of sight of my father. *Unter das Haus.*"

"Oh," said Revengo. By the tone he used Sandy knew that he didn't understand the German language at all and didn't get the meaning of *unter das Haus.* She was taking German in school, so she talked in it sometimes and taught Charmian some phrases. But Revengo had mixed her up so many times with the way he used words that she wouldn't even try to explain. It served him right not to know.

The girl took the setter out of the car in front of her house, waved good-bye to Mr. Revengo, and went up her steps pulling Rufus with her. She dragged him to a place alongside the house and said "Sit." Then she tried to push his hindquarters down. Rufus didn't sit. He stood wagging his tail that looked like a bunch of soft red feathers. Sandy shook her head. "Boy, you don't know one single thing about dog obedience, do you? You don't know how to walk on a leash without trying to kill a person off. You don't even know how to sit. I sure hope you know how to keep quiet because you're going to have to."

She bent down, then pulled Rufus around till he had his muzzle pointed toward a square black hole in the side of the house. She whispered, "That's *unter das Haus*. It means under the house. That's where you'll live till Sunday and the coast is clear over at Dad's school." She reached out her free hand to the side of the hole and took up the chrome-plated flashlight set beside it.

Rufus heard it switch on, and with the girl he watched its beam go over the two bowls put just inside the hole.

"Charmian did her part," Sandy told the dog. She clicked her tongue at him and pushed on his rear end, shoving him toward the hole.

Rufus resisted the pushing. He sat down now. Sandy sighed and, putting down the flashlight, reached in for one of the bowls. She held it under his snout. "Food," she told him.

The dog's nose told him "Meat!" It smelled wonderful. But the girl wouldn't put it down on the walk for him. No, she put it back into the hole. Rufus followed the bowl. An instant later Sandy Burns tossed his leash in after him, grabbed up the metal grating that fit over the hole, and slid it into place.

"Gotcha," she told the dog, as he whirled around and stuck his nose against the grating. Bending forward, her hands on her knees, Sandy added, "It's only till Sunday. My sister and I'll take you out for a walk tomorrow. Now you be a good dog. Don't bark and don't howl. Remember you're Mad McCormick's dog and that he's no friend to my dad. Be quiet now. Bark not. Howl not!"

Rufus didn't wait until she was out of sight around the garage door. He pushed at the grating with his nose. It didn't move. Then he tried to bite the grating. He couldn't get his teeth into the right position to do that. He put a paw on it and pushed. The grating rattled but held firm.

The rattling brought the vanilla girl back to the side of the house. She hissed at him, "Please keep quiet, Rufus McCormick."

He knew that tone and those words. He'd heard them from David McCormick often. David never yelled at him to be "quiet." He hissed the command when Rufus went with him to lecture halls. So now the dog went down onto his belly. He looked accusingly at the girl, who stood in the moonlight. Then he whined softly, but she didn't remove the grating and let him out. Instead, she went away again.

He was alone once more—but, no, not entirely alone! He lifted his head and listened. This wasn't like being tied to the Revengo's clothesline. There were voices overhead. Because of the voices he did not howl. He had never howled in the dormitory, where there were always voices around, though they were not always McCormick's.

For a time Rufus lay in the darkness looking wistfully out at liberty. And then he got up to wander around under the house. The first plumbing pipe he bumped his head against in the blackness made him go back to the grating again. From there he could see the outside, which lay in moonlight. All of this exercise had made him hungry. He lowered his head to the bowl of meat. It was "Beef Stew for Very Particular Cats," but that made no difference to him. What mattered was that it was very tasty. What was in the second bowl was a surprise. It wasn't water and it wasn't beer. Charmian Burns had forgotten that Sandy had wanted water put *unter das Haus*, and she had given Rufus milk, something he had not tasted since he was a puppy. He lapped all of it up.

3
UNTER DAS HAUS

Sandy came in the back door to find her mother and father waiting up for her as she'd expected. Her mother was putting a hem in a dress, and her father was soaking his feet in a tub while he watched the late news on TV. They both looked at her.

"You should get right to bed," said Professor Burns. "The Revengos stayed out pretty darned late tonight. Later than usual. It's eleven o'clock." He shot his daughter a sharp glance. "Revengo better fix that car door of his. It rattles. Somebody might fall out of it."

"I'll tell him," Sandy replied, knowing that the
rattling had been Rufus at the grating. Under her
breath she prayed that he wouldn't howl. He had
seemed to understand what *Be quiet*! meant. She
went to the refrigerator and poured herself a glass of
milk, then came back to the living room with it. She
could stay up a little longer if she was drinking milk.
Her parents let her do anything as long as she was
carrying a glass of milk. And she wanted to talk with
her father.

She asked, "How're you getting along these days
with Mad McCormick, Dad?"

He shifted his feet in the hot water. "Ah-h-h," he
muttered contentedly. "As of today, Mr. McCormick
is no longer my problem."

"Isn't he?" asked Mrs. Burns, who was brown-
haired, slim, and, like Sandy, not very tall. Her lanky
husband towered over both of them. "What happened today?"

Sandy listened intently. What had Rufus's owner
done now? It was clear to her that McCormick was in
really big trouble this time. If he hadn't been, she
doubted that her dad would have been so pleased.

Burns went on, almost purring, "At two P.M. today
Mr. McCormick left my life—forever, I trust. Forever, I hope."

"How did he do that?" asked Sandy.

Her father lifted a long white finger. "Let me re-
count the story to you. Yesterday I informed the
young man when he came to my office that he was to
get a D in English history, a grade he deserved. He

received a D on the examination paper and his book reports, so I must give him a D. He told me that I had 'shot down' his B average."

"Oh, dear," came from Mrs. Burns. "What did he say after that ?"

Burns laughed. "He didn't threaten me with a rope or a gun, but I suspect it entered his mind. He said something about 'really busting loose' and then he stormed out of my office. That was the last I saw of him until eleven o'clock this morning."

"What did he do then?" Mrs. Burns wanted to know.

"Did he bust loose?" asked Sandy, who was fascinated.

"He committed his first outrage of the day."

"He busted loose," said Sandra Burns.

"You might call it that."

"But what did he do?" asked Mrs. Burns.

"Have either of you ever seen a rubber chicken?"

"I eat them all the time in local restaurants, William," said his wife.

"Not that kind. I am speaking of a bird made out of rubber. It is the sort of thing that magic and joke shops sell, I believe."

"Like a little kid's bathtub toy, a rubber duck?" asked Sandy.

"Not in the slightest like a rubber duck. This is a horror, the same size as a real chicken without any feathers on it. It has the head and feet attached. In fact, it looks very much like a dead plucked chicken. Somehow McCormick got hold of a rubber chicken.

I suspect he borrowed it from another student. It seems to me that it would be the sort of gruesome item found in more than one student's closet in the dormitories."

"Dad, what did he do with it?"

"He smuggled it up into the top of the bell tower with him, and while a regent was addressing the faculty and students and the governor of California at the foot of the tower, he threw it down. I believe it was meant to land on my head, where I sat in the third row, to punish me for giving him a D and destroying his B average. It is my private opinion that Mr. McCormick was truly crazy at the moment."

"The chicken didn't land on you, Dad?" asked Sandy, clutching hard at the milk as she thought of Rufus *unter das Haus*.

"No, Mr. McCormick's aim was poor, or perhaps it was distorted by his anger. The chicken just missed the regent who was speaking. It hurtled past his shoulder, hit the concrete, and bounced up into the lap of the governor."

"Uh-huh, rubber bounces!" agreed Sandy.

Burns ignored her remark. "No one was amused. The regents did not appreciate the prank nor did the chancellor, and the governor was enraged. And then the chancellor recalled Mr. McCormick's climbing the bell tower last fall with a sign on his back telling the regents to go home. He sent the campus police who were on the edge of the crowd up into the bell tower after McCormick."

Sandy asked excitedly, "Did they catch him?"

"No, he had fled by that time. But they caught him at the scene of the next crime he committed."

"The next one?" asked Mrs. Burns.

"Yes. Something seemed to have snapped in his brain. From the bell tower he went to the campus radio station where minutes before the regents appeared he set off a smoke-making contraption. The radio station is a very small place, and the smoke was green. Like the library walls last year, the station will have to be repainted."

"Green?" put in Mrs. Burns, as she threaded her needle. "He really works at being Irish, doesn't he?"

"It would seem so. Even that dreadful dog he owns is an Irish setter. But Mr. McCormick will work at being Irish elsewhere from now on. The campus police caught him red-handed running away from the radio station. They escorted him to the chancellor's office."

"Did he say he threw the chicken and made the smoke, Dad?" asked Sandy.

"Oh, yes, from what I hear he was very open about it when the chancellor spoke to him later. McCormick said he was protesting the coming of the regents because they 'upset campus life too much.' "

Mrs. Burns asked, "What happened to the boy at two today?"

Professor Burns grinned with great satisfaction. "He was *expelled*. I presume that Mr. McCormick went back to his dormitory, packed up, and by this time has left the campus. I wouldn't be surprised if the campus police didn't escort him off it and perhaps drive him to the bus station. Perhaps he went home to his parents. I gather that his expulsion left him in a state of shock, although he's been asking for it. The faculty is lenient and gentle with students—particularly in the spring. But he went too far this time."

Expelled. Sandy's thoughts raced to the dog she had promised to shelter. "Where does McCormick live?" What if he had left town?

"I believe somewhere in central Texas. His parents, according to rumors I've heard, grow pecans. His scholarship is sponsored by the United Pecan Growers of America, so I imagine the story is true." Burns chuckled. "That could explain a great deal, I imagine. A childhood on a nut farm." Sandy's father stared gravely at her. "Why are you looking so mournful? Oh, I realize that the antics of Mr. McCormick might sound exciting, revolutionary, and glamorous to you, because you're young. He even entertained some of the faculty who didn't realize what he might be capable of. If David McCormick could have got hold of a man-eating shark, he might have put it into the campus swimming pool. That's where you and Charmian swim in the summer, remember."

"I remember." Sandy's mind was still on the dog under the house. What was she going to do about the dog now that McCormick had been expelled and forbidden the campus? Where was McCormick? Had he gone home to Texas? She couldn't ship Rufus off to him there. He hadn't gone to Mr. Revengo's to get his dog back, and he hadn't been to work at the pizza parlor tonight. No, he could have picked Rufus up any time after he'd been expelled that afternoon. Sandy knew about being expelled. Her boyfriend Eric had been threatened once for skipping classes at high school. Did McCormick's not coming after Rufus at the Revengo house mean what she was afraid it meant—that he had deserted his dog? That was a very bad thing to do.

Rufus might be homeless now.

After she finished the last of her milk, she told her father, "I guess McCormick wasn't a nice human being, huh?"

He said, "I am not even sure that he *was* a human being. Go to bed now. Don't wake Charmian up either."

Sandy rose from the sofa and went to the kitchen to rinse her empty glass. Maybe McCormick *had* been in a state of shock. States of shock sometimes meant that people's brains didn't work right. He might even have forgotten all about his dog being hidden out at Revengo's.

After saying good-night and brushing her teeth, Sandy went down the hall to the large bedroom she shared with Charmian.

A whisper greeted her out of its darkness. "Did you get the dog?"

"Uh-huh, he's *unter das Haus.*"

"I haven't heard any noises except a rattling and a bonging sound. It sounded like a pipe being hit by something."

"That was him," said Sandy, as she fumbled for her pajamas set out on the bed.

"What's the dog like, Sandy?"

"Big and red." Sandy wheezed with unhappiness. "I think he's going to be a real problem to us."

"How come?"

"Don't ask me now or you won't get another wink of sleep tonight. I'll tell you in the morning."

"Okay." Sandy heard her sister snuggling down under the covers. Then in a voice muffled by the sheet and blankets she always pulled over her head, Charmian added, "Hey, I think it's nice to have a dog—even if it's only for a little while."

"Don't be too sure of that," warned Sandy, as she took off her shoes. Suddenly she asked, "Where are the cats?"

"You mean are they outside or inside? They're inside." She giggled. "They're on Dad's bed waiting for him to come in and go to bed. You know, it's going on to midnight. That's where they always are at midnight."

"That's where they'd better be tonight, Char."

It smelled moldy under the house, and Rufus would have preferred a bed or a rug to the pebble-strewn dirt he was lying on. Yet he fell asleep almost at the moment Dr. and Mrs. Burns went to bed and the noise of footsteps over his head ceased. And he didn't let out one howl all night long, because he wasn't *truly* alone here! Many a time he'd been alone in McCormick's dormitory room, but there had been people all around him there, too. Here he could not only hear people's voices but could hear their footsteps.

Even if he couldn't see anyone, someone was up there. The girl who smelled like vanilla ice cream and who had given him the bowl of meat was there, for one. He'd recognized her voice through the floorboards.

The next morning at daybreak Rufus explored *unter das Haus.* By daylight he could see the plumbing pipes and avoid hitting them. He padded silently around under the house sniffing at this and that. Finally at the end of his tour of inspection, he heard voices directly overhead. One of them he recognized as belonging to Sandy. He hunkered down under the girls' bedroom floor, waiting for the sound of moving feet. When he heard them, he'd go back to the grating and wait to be let out and fed again.

Over his head Sandy was talking softly to Charmian. She wanted to explain matters before her parents got up. They liked to sleep late on Saturday mornings. "So Mad McCormick's gone away and Dad's glad."

"Whew!" Charmian breathed from her bed. "This is a mess. The dog hasn't got a home then. What're we going to do with him?"

Sandy said determinedly, "We're going to take him back to Mr. Revengo. That's where we got him."

"What if the Revengos don't want him?"

"Then we've got a bigger problem than we'd thought. Come on, get up. We'll go over to Revengo's right now with him."

"Right now?" squeaked Charmian, who liked to loll in bed, too, on Saturday mornings.

"Yeah, before Dad and Mother get up."

"Oh, okay." Charmian got out of bed and sat yawning on the edge. She was already wearing a blue sweatshirt and blue jeans. She jerked on her strawberry-blond braids to smooth them and reached for her tennis shoes beside the bed.

"Oh, my gosh, Char. What'd you do last night? Open your bed and fall into it?" asked Sandy.

"Yep."

"You'll smell."

"Oh, it's Saturday. Why don't you relax a little? You won't need any eye makeup at all until tonight. Even if you are going to see Earache before then, he won't mind. And I don't care if I smell."

"It's Eric. Eric Simpson. Not Earache."

Charmian laughed. "Earache is what Dad calls him when he gets you on the telephone for hours and hours. Old Earache S."

By now Sandy was into her own shirt, a green one, and dark green pants. There would be time only to grab a doughnut out of the refrigerator and get the dog. She peered at her blue eyes in the mirror. The mascara would have to wait, though she felt naked without it. But Eric wouldn't care. Sometimes he said she wore too much gunk on her face as it was. But he did like her to smell good, so she dabbled her vanilla-bean musk oil on her neck and wrists. It was impossible to reach the backs of her knees to perfume them, too, while she wore pants.

After Charmian had gone down the hall, Sandy started after her, carrying her heavy clogs in her hands. She didn't want her parents to hear her. Half-

way down the hall, she cracked a door and peered into
their bedroom. There they were, long forms under
the red blankets, each in his own twin bed. Beside her
father were two big gray lumps, the Burns's cats. She
thought to herself, In this corner we have Lady Jane
Grey weighing in at fourteen and a half pounds and
in that corner we have Mary Queen of Scots at fifteen
pounds even. And Dad called Mad McCormick nuts!
She shut the door quietly. It wouldn't do at all to
have one of the cats wake up and demand to be let
loose in the yard.

Charmian had a doughnut draped over one finger
and another sticking out of the side of her mouth.
She pointed her finger at Sandy, who slipped off the
doughnut ring on her way to the back door. They
went outside together and around the corner of the
house, where Sandy knelt down and whistled softly.
An instant later Rufus's shining black nose was at
the grating. "Good boy," said Sandy. She opened the
grating and grabbed for his collar as he emerged.

Delighted to see her, Rufus leaned against her to
be patted. Then he noticed taller Charmian and stood
still, gazing at her. "This is Char," Sandy told him.
"She's my sister. She smells, but she's not unkind."

"You're sure big and you're sure red," said Charmian patting Rufus, too.

He sniffed her. No, the other girl had the ice-cream
smell, not this one. This one smelled of tennis shoes
—and somewhat of cats. He accepted the chunk of
cinnamon doughnut Sandy held out to him and
wagged his tail, hoping for more food. But it wasn't

offered to him. Instead, the girl tugged at his leash. He sprinted forward alongside the house, dragging her down the steps to the sidewalk. She wanted to go for a walk!

Over her shoulder Sandy called out to Charmian, "He doesn't lead worth a dang!"

"Sure he does," Charmian yelled at her from the side of the house. "*He* leads. *People* follow! Hold him down for a minute till I get ready."

While Sandy struggled with Rufus on the sidewalk she wondered what Charmian was up to in the garage. She wasn't left in doubt very long. Charmian came sliding down the driveway on her shoe roller skates. She scooted by Sandy, and as she went past she grabbed the leash. "You get his collar and point him in the right direction, Sandy!" she called out.

Sandy yelled "Okay," caught at Rufus's collar, and pointed him eastwards. Running beside him, she and the dog leaped the curbing together. Hauled by Rufus, Charmian jumped it, landing with a jarring thud on her skates.

"Keep going," cried the younger girl. "Mush!"

Rufus had never pulled anyone on roller skates before. He felt a double tug on his collar, from the leash and along one side where Sandy held him. He was strangling slightly, but this was fun all the same. A new game! He ran where Sandy pointed him, and she ran beside him. They jumped two more curbs before they came to Blaine Street. And as they raced along, they were cheered by small neighborhood children out on their tricycles. An escort of small dogs followed them, yapping all the way to Blaine.

At Blaine Sandy called a panting halt. Blaine had quite a lot of traffic on it. She said to Charmian, "We'd better walk him across here, Char, and into the college housing development. Remember now, if we run into any regents, I'll say we're just visiting. If anybody says this is McCormick's dog, we'll deny it."

"Okay, shall we say he's Revengo's dog?"

"Heavens, no! That would get him into trouble. We'll say he's our dog."

"All right. I wish he were."

"Well, he isn't. Just keep that in mind!"

The two girls crossed properly in the crosswalk, looking both ways first. Two cars stopped to let them and Rufus go over. And then they were in the campus housing. They walked and skated with calm dignity, though Rufus strained heavily ahead of Sandy, who held his leash now.

While Charmian skated up and down the sidewalk in front of the Revengo house, Sandy rang the doorbell. After a time it was answered by the smallest Revengo child, who peeked out from behind the screen door, saw Rufus, and said, "Horsie."

Her father came after her wearing a purple and scarlet bathrobe. He looked rather sleepy. He gazed at Sandy, then down at the red dog. "Oh, my!" he said.

"You bet it's 'oh, my,' Mr. Revengo. My dad told me when I got home that Mad McCormick got expelled yesterday."

Mr. Revengo's eyes went to the ceiling of his porch. "Alas! I had not known this. Expelled. Oh, my!"

"Yes, alas, too. But it gets worse. He left the campus, according to Dad. I don't know where he went to. Has he been in touch with you?"

The man shook his head. "No. He did not come by, and he did not call me. He didn't bring a pizza to me for the dog last night at all."

"Pizza?" Sandy stared down at Rufus.

"Yes. Rumor has it that the dog was reared on pizza for the most part."

Sandy shook her head. Mad McCormick must have been really mad.

"He worked in a pizza parlor, you know," explained Revengo. "I suppose they gave him uneaten parts of pizzas, and he fed the dog on those."

"Oh," Sandy said. Then she went on, "Well, here's Rufus, Mr. Revengo. I've brought him back to you. Will you please unhook the screen door, or do you want me to take him around to the clotheslines again? Or do you want me to bring him back later when the regents are gone?"

The African let out his breath. "Sandy, I am afraid that I cannot take him even though the regents have come and gone. They inspected at an early hour."

"But McCormick brought him to *you*!"

Mr. Revengo spread out his hands. "The truth of the matter is that it would not be fair to the animal. This dog needs a home, a real home. You see I am getting my degree in June, which is next month. And then we are all going home to Africa. I cannot take the dog there. As I see it, he is homeless as of the moment."

"But you could take him until June and find a home for him then, couldn't you?" There was a desperate note in Sandy's voice.

"Not as easily as you might do it, Sandy. You live here. I am a stranger, a foreigner. You have contacts here in the town that I do not have." He added, "And perhaps McCormick might return. One never knows. Expelled students have been known to be reinstated. Who knows what might happen in the autumn or over the summer?"

Sandy nodded. Well, that was true. The only people Mr. Revengo knew were college people. She tightened her hold on the setter's collar. He was trying to rub noses with the smallest Revengo girl through the mesh of the screen door. She was cooing at him.

Sandy asked hopefully, "Maybe Mad McCormick's living here in town and still working at the pizza place? Is it the one on Iowa Avenue?"

"It is, indeed. Perhaps they might know about him there."

"Thank you, Mr. Revengo." Sandy pulled Rufus down the steps to where Charmian was skating in circles in the middle of the street, delighting four small children.

Detaching herself from them, Charmian asked, "What's up now?"

"We're going to the pizza parlor on Iowa, Char."

"Now? Nobody eats pizza for breakfast."

"That isn't why we're going there. I'll tell you on the way."

The pizza parlor was closed at this early hour of the day, but the manager was there. He came to the back door when Charmian yelled. Scenting pizza, Rufus made a lunge at the door, but the manager blocked it with great skill. He was a very large man and swift moving, too.

He looked at the girls and the red dog and listened to Sandy's story. Then he shook his head. "I fired McCormick night before last. He put mushrooms on a pepperoni pizza just one time too often. Mushrooms cost a lot of money. They belong on mushroom pizzas and nowhere else, unless the customer orders them specially on other pizzas. I don't know a confounded thing about McCormick's dog. I didn't even know he had a dog. I have no idea where McCormick lives now. And I don't care." He shut the door.

Out in front Charmian told her sister mournfully, "It looks as if we've got a dog on our hands."

Sandy said grimly, "I hope it's only temporary. I guess we'll have to take him back home and shove him *unter das Haus* again. It begins to seem that Rufus hasn't got a home."

"Getting him one will take some deep thinking," said Charmian. "He isn't a puppy anymore. I hear that people want puppies more than they want dogs."

"Yeah, they do," Sandy said in a sour tone. "Char, I guess we'll have to keep him while we think about people we know who might give him a place to live. It must be awful to be homeless! Even for a dog!"

4
DISCOVERIES

Disappointed because he hadn't received any pizza, Rufus didn't want to leave the pizza parlor. Sandy had to drag him away and push him on the rump, while Charmian pulled on his collar.

"Food, food!" cried Sandy. "We'll feed you when we get you back home."

"Yes, we'll raid the cat-food supply," came from Charmian.

The three of them went up Iowa Avenue. Rufus

went slinking and Sandy frowning. Charmian had to stumble along on her skates beside the road, because there were no sidewalks. Going up Blaine half a mile was just as bad because it had no sidewalks either. Worse than that, it was uphill all the way. By the time they'd reached the sidewalk part, they were all three out of breath and ready to stop at the red-roofed ice-cream and taco shack. Sandy had two quarters and Charmian eleven cents. That amount bought two soft ice-cream cones, with some change left over.

As the girls sat down at one of the little outside tables to do some deep thinking, Rufus let out a sudden whine. He put his paws onto the tabletop, snaked his head over toward Charmian, and took an enormous lick at her cone. Off went the whole top of it before she could jerk it away.

She laughed. "Hey, we know what else he likes beside pizza. Ice cream."

"And peanut butter and cat food and milk" Sandy added. "One thing about Rufus, he sure isn't finicky about his eating. That ought to make him attractive to somebody who needs a dog." She paused. "Okay, Char, let him have the rest of the ice cream. I'll go get you another one. Here's his leash. You hold him."

So Rufus devoured the remainder of Charmian's cone while she waited for her sister to get another for her. When Sandy came back with it, both girls ate their ice cream standing up to keep their cones out of the setter's reach.

Then home they went and together shoved Rufus once more *unter das Haus* after Charmian had brought out more cat food for him and this time filled his bowl with water, not milk.

"When twilight falls tonight, we shall walk you again," promised Charmian, who was feeling poetic at the moment. She was on her hands and knees peeking in at him as he pressed his nose to the grating. "Do not bark. Be quiet," she ordered him before she went away.

Rufus was quiet—until later that morning when four things happened. The clock in the living room bonged out eleven bongs over his head. The bongs woke Rufus up from the nap he had been taking. And an instant later a door opened and closed somewhere in the back of the house. The next thing was that he heard footsteps over his head. They were slower and heavier than Sandy's or Charmian's.

The last thing Rufus heard at a moment or two after eleven was a *put-put* sound somewhere out of sight. Then came a sort of sputtering roar from nearby. He waited with his nose to the grating for what interesting thing might happen next. What did occur was that a pair of large black boots walked by. The boots didn't stop; they went on to the garden gate, and the dog heard it creak open.

Then he heard Sandy's glad cry, "Eric."

Afterward came Charmian's greeting, "Ooooh, Earache."

"Hi," said a man's voice. Rufus pricked his ears forward. The voice wasn't one he recognized, but it was a nice one. A student's voice. He listened, but it didn't come again.

Instead, he heard Sandy talking. "Hey, Eric, wait'll you see what we've got *unter das Haus.*"

Eric laughed. "Something German, huh?"

"Nope," said Charmian. "Something Irish, but it's red. It isn't one bit green."

The boy said, "Let's see it. Let's drag it out by the heels and destroy it before I mow the lawn for your folks. That's me, Eric, the dragon slayer."

"No, no, Earache. It's a nice something," said Charmian.

The voices were nearing his grating now. Rufus heard the gate shut, and in front of him he saw Sandy's and Charmian's shoes and the black boots.

However, behind them, rising up out of the ice plant, he spied something else. It was a large gray cat, striped like a tiger, its eyes blazing a furious jade green. It stood motionless behind the three pairs of legs. Motionless—but its tail was switching back and forth as it peered through them at the dog imprisoned under the house. All at once it let out a hiss like an angry snake.

Charmian was first to become aware of the creature. Rufus heard her soft wail, "Hey, there's Mary Queen of Scots. She's spotted Rufus. Dad must have let the cats out the front door without our knowing it."

The Irish setter heard Sandy draw her breath in and her low words, "Oh, Lord, there's Lady Jane Grey. She's right behind her."

And now a second cat, equally large, jade-eyed and tiger-striped, came slinking up to stand beside the other. Both tails were switching. Lady Jane Grey didn't hiss. She snarled and stepped forward on stiff legs. Then she crouched down under the clothesline with her eyes on Rufus.

Rufus growled. He paid no attention to the large boy with dark curling hair and black vinyl jacket who was hunched over staring in at him through the grating. The dog's eyes were fixed on the cats in deadly hatred.

"Get the cats out of here," Eric Simpson told Sandy and Charmian. "This dog's going to make a break for it any minute!"

"We can't," wailed Sandy. "They'll scratch us. They're too big. It'd be like picking up barbed wire."

"Then we'd better get out of their way," ordered the boy. Grabbing a girl by each arm, Eric propelled them into the garage.

The cats were both crouched down now making horrible threatening noises as they tried to stare Rufus down. Four green eyes glared into one pair of brown. Rufus took up their challenge. With a shrill bark he flung himself hard against the grating. It didn't give way, but one of the metal fasteners that held it to the side of the house snapped off. Barking frantically he squeezed past the grating that had slid to one side. His leash trailing, the red dog dashed at the cats.

They were fast, those two. Over the wooden gate they went, a flickering of striped gray tails, one after the other. Over the gate Rufus went also—scrabbling with his claws, teetering on its top until he slid down the other side. His leash scudding along the concrete, he streaked over the patio in pursuit of the cats. The Burnses' yard was a large one. Around and around the sycamore and the fruitless mulberry tree they ran —two cats and the Irish setter. And then the cats separated. Mary Queen of Scots ran off leaping through the center of the tiny flowering plum, scattering pink blossoms over the lawn. Barking, Rufus chased her up the mulberry tree from there. She perched at the tree's top, squalling. Lady Jane Grey an instant later darted under the badminton net. Following her, Rufus ran into the net and brought it down on his head. This obstruction gave Lady Jane Grey time to jump up into the planter that held Mrs. Burns's roses and from there over the fence into the neighbor's backyard. She raced across that and disappeared into a clump of oleanders.

Rejoicing in his victory, Rufus dashed about the yard four times yelping, his tongue lolling between yelps. He'd lost the entangling badminton net during the first victorious run around the yard, but his leash still followed him. Finally he stopped and stood waiting until the Burns girls and Eric came up to him. But they didn't pat him on the head and praise him the way McCormick always did when he chased a campus cat out of sight.

"Oh, boy," said Charmian, "are you ever in big trouble now, dog!"

And at that very moment the glass sliding door at

the rear of the Burnses' house opened. Professor
Burns, in a faded orange bathrobe, came out to stand
on the stoop. Out of another door, the study door,
stepped Mrs. Burns in a long pale blue robe. Burns
spoke first. He stabbed a long finger at Rufus sitting
in the middle of the lawn. His voice was a dull roar.
"What is that?"

"It's a dog, sir," Eric Simpson told him.

"You have quick wits, Earache," came from Charmian.

"For the information that I am looking at a dog,
I thank you, Eric," said Professor Burns. He demanded of all three, "Now, tell me, just what has
happened to the cats?"

Sandy pointed to the mulberry tree. "Mary Queen
of Scots is up there. You can't see her, but you can
hear her, Dad. Lady Jane Grey went over the fence.
They're both okay."

"Are you sure?" called out Mrs. Burns, worried.

"Sure, I'm sure, Mother. We saw it all. They're
just fine."

Professor Burns came down off the stoop in his
bathrobe and bedroom slippers. As he came, he was
peering through his glasses. Halfway up to the two
girls and Eric and the panting dog he took off the
glasses, wiped them with a handkerchief from his
bathrobe pocket, then put them back on. Suddenly
he stopped in his tracks. For the second time he
pointed. In a very strange voice, which sounded like
a gurgle, he said, "My God, I think that animal is
Mad McCormick's dog!"

Sandy answered swiftly. "It is. But he can't help it, Dad." She had decided to appeal to her father's sense of fair play. She'd explain everything to him.

But he wouldn't give her the chance. "What's *he* doing *here*?" he thundered.

"Seeking sanctuary. He's been abandoned by Mr. McCormick," she explained.

Eric took the explanation up too. "Left without food or water or loving friends."

"Dumped," summed up Charmian. A second later she added, "Homeless, too."

"All three of you have been reading your mother's novels," replied Professor Burns. "You didn't make up that dialogue. Someone else did. Don't try to get around me. How did you come by McCormick's animal? I know him by sight all too well. That dog sat on the floor in front of me, staring at me, during one whole lecture, as if I'd just got off a spaceship from Venus. It was very annoying, let me tell you. I don't think he even blinked." Burns gave Rufus a glance that sent the dog down into a nerveless slump on the grass. The man's eyes were stabbing holes through everyone in sight except his wife. He asked Eric. "Simpson, did *you* bring him here?"

"No, Dad, I did. Oh, please let me tell you about it."

And while her father frowned Sandy explained how she'd got the dog from Mr. Revengo. She added, "Mr. Revengo's leaving so he can't keep him."

Mrs. Burns had come out in the yard, too. She

shook her head after she'd heard Sandy's story. "Sandra, you should have told us you brought the dog home last night and put him under the house. It wasn't one bit fair, you know."

"How come it wasn't fair?" asked Charmian.

"Because our cats are old ladies. They shouldn't be hounded by dogs. They're nearly twelve years old, remember. They can't run up trees and jump fences the way they used to."

"They did just fine today, Mrs. Burns. They're in great shape," stated Eric.

"Enough of this," said Professor Burns. "I must say that I am sorry for this homeless dog, who seemed to find me so fascinating. It's too bad that Mr. McCormick didn't pay half as much attention to my lecture. Certainly I am truly sorry for anything that has borne the brunt of Mr. McCormick. But we are not going to keep this animal. I know what you are trying to do—play on my sympathies and get me to tell you that he can live here with us. He cannot. You will have to find a home for him—elsewhere."

"But why?" asked Charmian. "He's a great watchdog! Look at the way he chased the cats just now." She stopped to pat Rufus, who licked at her fingers.

"The cats *live* here, Charmian. The dog *does not*," Professor Burns corrected her.

"Why can't we keep him?" asked Sandy. "He can live under the house and be an outside dog. It never gets cold here in Southern California really. He can make friends with the cats."

"No, Sandra." As Rufus stared up at the hard-voiced man who hadn't once patted him, Professor Burns went on, "Besides we are going away—all four of us in June."

"Huh?" said both girls together.

"Uh-huh," Burns mocked them. "I didn't tell you before because I didn't want to have to hear you, Sandra, complain that you're going to miss summer school and you, Charmian, that you won't be going to Camp Tautona. We're all going to England."

"No!" said Charmian loudly.

"No," said Sandy softly.

Eric said not a word. His face changed, though. Sandy was his girl, and she was going away. He squatted beside Rufus and put an arm around the dog's neck. Rufus licked his cheek. Eric smelled of food, of vanilla ice cream, too. Eric and Sandy used the same vanilla-bean musk oil but Eric put it on his hair. All the same his face smelled good.

Professor Burns paid no attention to Eric or to the Irish setter. He spoke to his daughters over the sound of Mary Queen of Scot's hissing. His voice came rather close to hissing too. "I have made the decision. I am tired of feeling hagridden. I have a wife, two daughters, two female cats, and even a female palm tree out in front of the house. As I said, we are going to England in June. We won't be back here until late September. The dog cannot go to England."

Mrs. Burns added, "Girls, if it makes you feel any better, the cats won't be going with us either."

Professor Burns said, "Quite true. The people who

take care of the house for us will look after the cats and feed them."

"Dad, you'd dump Lady Jane Grey and Mary Queen of Scots in their old age?" asked Sandy slyly.

"Yes, I would. Your mother is quite right. There's a quarantine law in the British Isles pertaining to dogs and cats. Any dog or cat seeking to enter Great Britain must spend six months in quarantine. We'll only be there a little over three months. I suspect the cats will be all right. It isn't forever and ever, you know."

"No, it will only seem that way," said Charmian. Then she asked, "But they let people in, don't they? People carry diseases, too."

"The English seem to worry more about animals than they do about people," said Mrs. Burns.

Professor Burns shook his head. "I don't make the laws in the British Isles, but I like to think I make them in this household now and then." He came closer to loom over Rufus and Eric. "Simpson, you'd better mow the lawn and then weed the rose beds."

"But what'll we do with the dog?" asked Sandy.

"I do not care," replied her father. "I think if I were you I'd call the Humane Society right now."

"No, sir," Eric said loudly. He lumbered to his feet. "No, sir, nobody has to do that." With his hand protectively on Rufus's collar, Eric went on, "I'll take care of him!"

"Oh, Eric," breathed Sandy.

Professor Burns said nothing more. He went back into the house, and Mrs. Burns followed him with only a shake of her head at her daughters and Sandy's boyfriend.

"Earache, I love you too," cried Charmian. She flung her arms around the boy.

"Spare me the wild crushes of junior-high girls like you," Eric said. He stood looking down at the red dog. "What am I going to do with you? I've already got a dog. My mother probably won't want another." He looked at Sandy. "Why do you suppose I said that I'd take him? I must be nuts."

"No, you aren't. It's because you're noble and good." Sandy kissed him on one cheek at the same moment that Rufus reared up and licked him on the other.

"Hey, what's all this love stuff about?" asked Eric, twisting away from both girl and dog.

"Rufus *knows*. That's what it's all about," Charmian told him, as she went to stand under the mulberry tree preparatory to climbing it to get Mary Queen of Scots down.

"Well, what does he know? What does a dog know?" Eric asked her.

"Dogs recognize the people who are noble and nice. That's what they know," she told him.

"Oh, baloney, they don't either," said Eric. But all the same he looked quite pleased at the compliments. And he didn't wipe off either cheek with the sleeve of his coat.

"Eric, do you suppose you could go slowly enough on your motorcycle for Rufus to run home beside you later on today?" asked Sandy.

"Yeah, I guess my cycle could go that slow."

"Well, that's good. It's too long to your house for us to walk him over."

"What will your mother say about Rufus?" cried Charmian halfway up the tree.

Eric spoke calmly, giving the dog's leash to Sandy. "Tie him to the clothespole for me, please, while I get out the power mower."

Sticking her head out of the tree, Charmian called down to him. "You didn't answer my question. What about your mother?"

"Well, I don't intend to take him home to my old lady at all. I'm going to take him to my Aunt Fern. She lives alone on Lime Street downtown. I think she ought to have a watchdog. Maybe she'll give him a home."

"Oh, no. Not her!" moaned Sandy.

Eric shrugged. "Why not? It's any old port in a storm for Rufus right now, isn't it?"

"Gosh, Eric, she's an awful old port," Sandy told him, shaking her head so hard her hair fluffed out around her. She looked sadly at Rufus. "You know in his own way, he's a darling."

Rufus caught the magic word. Up came the right front paw to be shaken.

"Look. He know's he's a darling," she said delightedly, as she took the paw and shook it. She looked up at Eric, who was grinning at the setter. "But will your Aunt Fern like him? She's rather strange, Eric."

"Rather!" he snorted.

5
MISS SIMPSON

At four o'clock Sandy went coasting on her ten-speed behind Eric's red motorcycle down Blaine Street. Beside the cycle at the very far right of the road trotted the Irish setter on his leash. At times he made gagging sounds, not because Eric went too fast for him but because the cycle's exhaust smelled so bad. Rufus didn't take one single playful nip at the bottoms of Eric's jeans. The smell and the noise the cycle made were too much for him. Sandy, too, was making gagging noises by the time they turned right off

Blaine onto Lime Street two miles from her home.

Miss Simpson lived four houses down Lime on the left side of the street. She owned the little house. A retired schoolteacher, she liked everything to be neat. Because the house was on Lime Street it was painted green, a pale green. It had a dark green roof and an even darker green trim around the windows. The lawn was green velveteen dichondra. The birdbath out front, though, was just gray concrete.

Eric stopped the motorcycle and waited for Sandy to put her ten-speed up on the sidewalk. Then he got off the cycle and arranged the kickstand.

"I'm scared," Sandy told him, as he took the setter by the collar. "Eric, I think you should have called your aunt on the phone first. People like to be warned sometimes."

"She would have said no right out if I had, Sandy. We have to try her out without warning her. It's the best way." Frowning, Eric took Rufus up onto the front porch and rang the doorbell.

Rufus sniffed the porch. He couldn't smell anything but the dirt in the wooden tubs set on each side of the door. The plants growing inside the tubs didn't seem to have any smell at all. Miss Simpson's night-blooming cacti hadn't bloomed for two years in a row. Rufus pressed forward as he heard the sound of footsteps coming toward him. They were light steps, high-heeled ones.

The door opened a crack, and a woman peered out. A gush of flower-smelling perfume came ahead of her. Rufus sneezed. He'd smelled that before. The campus had been planted with jasmine bushes. Every time he went to roll in the jasmine bushes he sneezed.

"Hi, Aunt Fern," said Eric, "Sandy and I have brought you a present."

"You have, Eric? How very nice of you, darling," the woman said with a laugh.

At the word *darling* Rufus lifted a paw. No one took it to shake, but he kept it in the air all the same. And then Eric's aunt opened her door further. Rufus surged ahead of Eric, trying to get in.

"No," cried the thin, little white-haired woman. "Leave the dog outside, please."

"Aunt Fern, he *is* the present," explained Eric.

"A dog?" Aunt Fern looked out of bright blue eyes at Rufus. "A dog?" she repeated. She lifted her gaze to her nephew. "Eric, you know I like birds, but I've never had a dog in all my life."

Eric pushed past her into the living room, taking Rufus with him. Sandy followed behind them, nodding at Miss Simpson as she did. Eric headed directly for the purple velvet sofa and sat down. Rufus didn't sit. When Sandy seated herself beside Eric, both of them forced the red dog down onto his rear. Miss Simpson came from the door to lower herself into a violet upholstered rocking chair.

Everyone was silent.

Rufus sniffed the house. There was not only the smell of jasmine perfume here. There was something more—something musty and musky. He didn't begin to know what the smells could be. He whimpered, but Eric hushed him.

Sandy snuggled nearer Eric. Miss Simpson had always scared her a little. She was 'into" things that the girl didn't understand. There were tarot cards and a crystal ball on the little round table set between the sofa and the four chairs in the tiny living room. Miss Simpson's house always smelled of sandalwood incense and musky birdcages and birdseed. Right now her mynah bird was in the living room. He seemed to be asleep in his tall, gold-colored cage. At least he was sagging on his perch.

The mynah bird, Ali, made Sandy more nervous than anything else. Miss Simpson had let him out of his cage once when she had come visiting with Eric. The big black bird had flapped across the room straight at her. In mid-flap he'd dropped down to her shoulder, digging in his claws.

"Don't move," Eric had told her. So she hadn't. She'd sat like a statue while Ali had pecked at one of her silver hoop earrings, making it swing back and forth until he was weary of the game. Would he peck her ear or her cheek? Finally he'd released his claws and flopped his awkward way onto the table to peer at his reflection in the crystal ball.

"Ali likes you. Ali knows," the woman had told Sandy then.

"Is my shoulder bleeding?" Sandy had asked Eric later, while the mynah went on admiring himself in the crystal ball and Miss Simpson had gone to the kitchen to make a cup of peppermint tea for her guests.

"No." Eric had put his arm around her and given

her a quick bear hug. "Ali really must like you. He didn't sink his claws in. And he flew to you. He really raked me last year, and he didn't fly over to me either. He sort of walked up me to get onto my shoulder."

Now Sandy looked down at Rufus wondering if Ali would like him, too. The mynah was spooky. So was Miss Simpson. Rufus might be crazy, but he wasn't spooky. Sandy wanted to get up and leave, but she couldn't. She'd just had one of those "insights" her psychology· teacher was always talking about. A person or an animal could be nutty and not one bit spooky.

Miss Simpson was leaning forward in her chair. Her white hands were clasped over the knees of her green caftan. "Now, Eric, why are you bringing me this dog as a present?"

"Because you live alone and you need a watchdog, and because he needs a home. This is Rufus."

"He's an Irish setter," put in Sandy. She patted Rufus whose nose was still twitching while he sampled the odd scents of the house. She was about to go on and say that she thought he might be pedigreed when a loud cawing interrupted her.

Ali had come to sudden life. The three people and Rufus tilted their heads to look up at the cage in the corner. The mynah had come nearer to the side of the cage facing Rufus. He slid even closer along his perch and looked down at the setter with his head cocked on one side. His bright eyes stared down into Rufus's. For a long moment there was another dead silence while Miss Simpson held the index finger of one hand to her lips and pointed to Ali with the index finger of the other.

Suddenly Ali let out a loud hiccup. Following that came the very loud words, "You, sir, are a dirty cur."

Rufus had never heard a bird talk before. He jerked to his feet and barked, but his barking could not drown out the mynah's screeching, "Dirty cur. Dirty cur."

When the mynah bird stopped, Eric managed to quiet Rufus by putting one hand over the dog's jaws and clamping his mouth shut. It had taken a good deal of Eric's strength to keep Rufus from leaping at the cage. And Eric Simpson was not puny. He lifted weights for a hobby, and when he didn't have any weights he ran up and down the steps of their high school carrying Sandy, who weighed an even hundred pounds. Eric watched his weight to see that he didn't get over two hundred pounds and watched hers to see that she didn't get over or under an even hundred.

Eric stood with both hands on the dog's back, holding him down even though Rufus wasn't barking anymore. "I guess it won't work, Aunt Fern. Ali doesn't like him."

"Oh, but it might work out just fine. Sit down, darling," ordered Miss Simpson.

Eric forced Rufus down, and Rufus raised a paw. Sandy shook it because no one else seemed to be about to. She was sorry for Rufus—even sorrier now that Miss Simpson might give him a home.

The woman went on. "Ali is a fine judge of character. Calling someone a dirty cur is something of a compliment from him. He calls some of my best friends that." She laughed. "You should hear what he called the man who came here asking me to marry him last month."

"What did he call him?" Eric asked politely, but hopefully, Sandy thought.

"Something in the Hindi language. I did not catch the exact meaning, but Ali was hatched and raised in India, remember. I understood the gist of it. Ali didn't approve of the man so I refused him. I had always suspected him of being a fortune hunter anyway."

"Oh," was Eric's disappointed comment. He was silent for a moment, fondling Rufus's ears. Then he asked, "Ali's pretty valuable, isn't he?"

"Oh, yes, worth several hundred dollars."

"And how about the birds in your bedroom and in the dining room, Aunt Fern?"

"Even if they're still moulting, most of them, they're worth quite a bit of money—the lovebirds in particular." She glanced at Sandy, who blushed. Miss Simpson guessed how she and Eric felt about each other.

"Then you need a watchdog to guard the birds, Aunt Fern," Eric told her.

"Perhaps so." Miss Simpson looked at Rufus. As she did she wrinkled her forehead. "I hope he eats food other than meat. I am a vegetarian, you know."

"Rufus was raised on pizza. It comes in a cheese flavor," Sandy put in quickly, as she stooped to pat Rufus on the rump. He was still staring transfixed at

Ali's cage as if he dared the bird to speak again. "He likes peanut butter and ice cream, too."

"Well," said Aunt Fern, "that is rather unusual, isn't it?" She shook her head. "I do wish he weren't red. I would have preferred another color. He clashes with my house."

"He won't be in it if he's to be a watchdog, Aunt Fern. He'll be outside," Eric said. "Anyhow he'd be happier in the yard."

"More than likely he would." Miss Simpson nodded. "All right, Eric, I'll take him. What did you say his name was?"

"Rufus."

"Oh." The woman closed her eyes as she sat rigid in her chair, her hands tight on its arms. All at once she relaxed, startling Sandy Burns. "I like the name well enough, but if he works out well here, I may give him another. Something Gaelic naturally. Perhaps Shawn or Padraic or something of that ilk."

"Sure, Aunt Fern." Eric got up. "Shall I take the dog to the backyard now?"

"Yes, take him out the front way and through the gate." She followed Sandy and Eric and Rufus out onto the porch, then she asked, "Eric, does the dog have his dog license?"

"No," Sandy called back over her shoulder, as Eric hauled Rufus down the steps. Rufus was twisted around, looking longingly toward the mynah bird inside the house.

"What about his rabies shots, Eric?" the woman called out, as they went around the side of the house.

"Probably not, Aunt Fern."

Miss Simpson's voice floated after them. "Then I'll take him to the veterinarian, and he'll have a complete physical examination and get his shots."

"My gosh," Sandy told Eric, as he fumbled with the latch of the gate, "one minute your aunt's way out and the next minute she's with things all the way."

Eric replied as he snapped the leash off Rufus's collar and pushed him through the open gate, "I know. That sort of thing runs in my dad's family. That's why he and Mom split up a long time ago. She could never figure him out. He kept changing all the time."

While Sandy clicked the gate shut behind the dog she tried not to feel guilty about Rufus. She wasn't at all sure that he would work out with Miss Simpson— not after having lived on the campus with Mad McCormick.

"Eric, you'll come visit Rufus, won't you?" she asked, as the two of them went back to the front porch to drop the leash onto the doormat. Miss Simpson had gone inside.

"Sure. I mow Aunt Fern's back lawn every Sunday afternoon for her." He put his arm around Sandy. "How do you suppose I get the money to take you out on Saturday nights?"

"You are really nice and noble, Eric Simpson."

"And you are acting like a gooshy teeny bopper, Sandra Burns. Aunt Fern won't mind if you come visit the dog on Sundays while I'm working." He laughed. "She likes me. Did you notice how she calls

me 'darling'? She phoned Mom once to say that I was
of good moral character because I didn't weed lying
down. The last guy who did her yard used to bring
a radio with him. He'd lie down on his stomach beside it and listen while he pulled up dandelions. That
bothered her."

Rufus realized shortly that he didn't like the yard
he was confined in one little bit. In the first place it
was much too small. In the second place it was full of
stuff—a lawn swing, iron table and chairs, benches,
and in the center another birdbath. Where there
wasn't furniture, there were trees. Big pepper trees
with long trailing lacy branches that struck him on
the nose, tickling it, when he wandered about. Herb
plants bordered the little flagstone walk. To Rufus's
inquiring nose some of them smelled dreadful. He did
not like rosemary or sage. But the fourth thing was
worst of all. The fence. Miss Simpson's fence wasn't
a chain-link fence, the kind a dog could peer through.
It wasn't even the sort of picket fence that would go
nicely with the little green house. No, this was
a seven-foot tall solid redwood fence some former
owners had built a long time ago. It was much too
tall to leap over. No one could look out. No one
could peek in. Rufus couldn't even find a knothole
in it at the proper level for him to stare out at people
passing up and down Lime Street.

And he was *alone*. Absolutely *alone*! No comforting human voices and no footsteps anywhere. Fifteen
minutes after Eric and Sandy had left him, Rufus sat

himself down next to the birdbath, lifted his head to the sky, and let out a long quivering howl. It was one of pure loneliness and misery. It rose agonizingly throughout the neighborhood time and time again. He followed this series of howls by three more very loud heartbreaking ones. Upstairs windows were flung open in the houses on both sides of Miss Simpson's. People looked out of them as the setter let out a series of yelps intermixed with howls.

Finally the back door of Miss Simpson's house opened, and she came out. She stood frowning at Rufus, who got to his feet in mid-yelp and came over to her, with her finger to her lips for silence. Not even patting him on the head, she went back into the house and shut the door almost on Rufus's nose. At his bark of protest, she stuck her head out and told him, "You hush up now. I'll be back in a jiffy."

And she was, carrying a pan of water, which she put down. Rufus drank it. Then she brought out a second pan. "It's macaroni and cheese from last night's supper," she told the dog. "Eric did say you liked cheese." Then she went inside again.

For a time after he'd eaten the macaroni and cheese, Rufus waited hopefully beside the back door. He wanted someone to come out and keep him company, but no one did. His head drooping, he padded back to the birdbath and took up his station for the night.

Alone once more! *Totally alone!* He began to howl again, though sometimes just for variety he let out a frantic yelping.

The windows that had been closed opened again. A woman's voice called out, "Miss Simpson, have you got a dog? I can't see it because of the pepper trees. But I can hear it!"

Rufus saw one of Miss Simpson's windows being pushed open. He saw her put her head out. "What did you say, Mrs. Curtis?"

"Have you got a dog?"

"*No!*" And the Simpson window was cranked shut.

"Well, I never!" came from the neighbor, who slammed her window down.

Once this exchange had taken place, Rufus started to howl again. Until midnight he howled and yapped and yelped. When the moon rose over the pepper trees, he bayed at it. Morning found him very weary and slumped down beside the birdbath.

As for the people on that block of Lime Street, no one slept a wink all night either.

Miss Simpson had lain awake in her bed, too. She'd put earplugs into her ears and had even taken a sleeping pill. Nothing could make her drowsy. And the sight of her bedroom telephone off the hook to block the neighbors' incoming calls made her feel very guilty.

What on earth was the matter with that dog? Why should he howl so? Other people's dogs got along just fine living in backyards. Wasn't he a watchdog at heart? Did he expect to be in the house sleeping on her bed?

At nine o'clock Sunday morning she made her

breakfast of sassafrass tea and wheat-germ cereal, ate it, and gave Rufus the last of the macaroni and cheese.

At nine thirty she called a friend across town. "Dear, do you remember telling me about a man who understands animals? You were talking about him when we had lunch together last week."

Miss Simpson listened intently to the answer, then said into the phone, "Didn't you say he was coming here very soon to demonstrate?" There was a silence, then Miss Simpson said, "Oh, very good! Monday night at the YMCA at seven thirty. I'll be there." Another pause. "No, dear. It isn't Ali or any other bird I'm worried about, though I do have a canary that's never sung a note. Thank you. Good-bye."

She was out watering her herb garden when Eric and Sandy arrived at two o'clock that afternoon. Happy now that he had company, Rufus was lolling in the sunshine. His eyes were on the garden hose. He hoped that the woman would squirt him. But she hadn't even patted him or called him by name. As a matter of fact, she had treated him in a very cold manner.

Miss Simpson greeted Eric and Sandy as they came in the gate with, "That dog howled all night long. All of the neighbors are furious with me because of him. So I've decided to take him to see the Man from Monrovia tomorrow evening."

"Is he some kind of vet, Aunt Fern?" Eric wanted to know.

"No, but he understands animals. He's to be at the YMCA tomorrow night at seven thirty. Eric, would you and Sandra like to go there with me and this dog?"

Eric shrugged his big shoulders. "I guess so." He look at Sandy. "How about it? You can do your math homework right after you get home from school, huh?" He turned to his aunt. "What does this guy do? Is he going to examine Rufus?"

"No, according to my friend he's only going to talk with the dog, darling."

Darling! Tired as he was, Rufus got up and lifted a paw. Sandy was staring at Eric and Eric at his aunt. Nobody at all was looking at him to take his paw.

"Talk?" Sandy whispered to her boyfriend.

6
THE MAN
FROM MONROVIA

Regaining his strength after eating five soybean steaklets that evening, Rufus yelped and howled from darkness Sunday night till dawn. Miss Simpson gritted her teeth and kept her phone off the hook again. She did not answer her doorbell, though it rang often that night.

"I'll pin my hopes to the Man from Monrovia," she told herself over and over again.

Sandy and Eric came *put-putting* up together on

Eric's motorcycle to the house on Lime Street at seven ten Monday night. Sandy wasn't so sure about going to the Y with Eric and his aunt and Rufus. She leaned back against the sissy bar of Eric's cycle and said, "I'm not so sure we ought to do this. Sounds sort of crazy, doesn't it?"

"Uh-huh." Sometimes Eric was a man of few words. "Come on," he told her. "Get off and I'll put the cycle in the backyard so nobody'll steal it. You go tell Aunt Fern that we're here if she can hear you over the dog's howling."

The girl got off the cycle and went slowly up the front porch, her hands deep in the pockets of her jeans. She had no idea how to dress to go hear a man who talked with animals, so she'd worn her best jeans, the pair with embroidery and rhinestones on them and her khaki Army jacket with her name embroidered in pink cross-stitch across the back.

She rang the doorbell reluctantly while she listened to Rufus yelping now in the backyard.

"Who's there?" came a shrill voice that didn't sound much like Miss Simpson.

"Me, Sandy Burns. Me and Eric."

"Oh, yes." Miss Simpson didn't even correct Sandy's grammar.

Then there was a rattling of a chain, and the door opened a little bit. The woman peered out. She sighed with relief and opened the door further. Immediately she stuck out her hand and gave Sandy the dog leash. "Please tell Eric to secure that animal for me and lead him out, and you come inside, dear."

"Sure." Sandy took the leash and, standing on the front porch, flung it to Eric, who was pushing his cycle into the backyard. He caught it with one hand. Sandy called, "She wants you to drag Rufus out front."

"Okay," Eric grunted. Then he yelled, "Hey, Rufus, shut up. I'm coming."

An instant later, the howling stopped. There came one joyful bark and blessed quiet. Sandy grinned. All was well. The red dog had found Eric, who knew about dogs. She took a deep breath and went inside the living room through the open door. It was different now. The mynah bird wasn't there. Even his cage was gone.

"Where's Ali?" the girl asked, as Miss Simpson screwed on her earrings in front of the living-room mirror.

Tonight she was wearing a long white dress with lavender and blue daisies all over it. A purple shawl was thrown over her nearby violet rocker. The smell of jasmine was very strong about her.

"I had to put Ali into the bathroom. It's painted dark green so it has a very calming effect. I spent all last night in there trying to calm Ali while that dog howled." Miss Simpson's hands were shaking as she picked up the shawl. "My dear, you should have heard what Ali said last night. No, on second thought, you should not have heard it."

"Did he say it in Hindi or in English?"

Miss Simpson compressed her lips. "In English,

unfortunately. I wasn't aware that Ali knew such words."

"Maybe he lived in England, too, after he was hatched?"

"Perhaps. I do not know all of his history." She tilted her head to one side in a manner Sandy found birdlike. "Come to think of it, Ali did have something of an English accent last night."

"How are the other birds?"

"Nervous wrecks. Pecking at each other, not eating. They simply are not used to so much uproar." Miss Simpson started for the door, carrying her shawl. "Are you ready, Sandra?"

"I guess so."

"Well, come along then, or we'll be late. We'll walk. It's only six blocks from here. I'll make a donation for the four of us."

Eric was ready on the sidewalk with Rufus in tow. Rufus ran for Sandy, put his paws on her shoulders, and touched his nose to the vanilla girl's. She hugged him about his middle. Boy, had he ever had a gruesome time lately! Deserted by Mad McCormick, rejected by her father, and now about to meet a man who might do something awful to his brain. Or whatever the Man from Monrovia did.

They walked together across Lime, going straight ahead with Rufus leading Eric, who felt the strain in his arm muscles by the time the dog had hauled him four of the six blocks to the YMCA. They were late, not because of Rufus but because of Miss Simpson, who was always a bit late wherever she went. The big room at the Y was packed, not just with people but with animals!

While Sandy hunted for seats in the rear of the hall, Eric, Rufus, and Miss Simpson stood in the doorway. There Miss Simpson stuffed four one-dollar bills into a box marked *Donations*.

Rufus's nose scented the place as Sandy went up and down the aisles. It smelled like nothing he had ever smelled before except perhaps a campus laboratory. Once McCormick had taken him to the psychology lab, which had held rats and monkeys. They had not smelled good, though they had smelled interesting. Now the hair on Rufus's back started to rise. He could smell rats, but there were other odors, too. Dogs and cats—and other things as well. And there were sounds, too. Small snufflings and mewings and rustling, slithering sounds. Something was squeaking at the moment. Rufus let out a growl.

"It's okay, Rufus," said Eric, patting him and at the same time getting a firmer grip on his collar.

"Oh, hush up, dog," came from Aunt Fern. She shook her finger at Rufus. "It's for your own good that we brought you here." Suddenly she stood on tiptoe and waved. She grabbed at Eric's arm. "Look, there's Sandra waving at us. She's got seats for us way down in front. See, she's signaling for us to come on."

"Oh, my Lord, way down in front! I hope it isn't the front row," muttered Eric, as his aunt sailed out ahead of him. He gave Rufus a nudge. But Rufus wouldn't move. Eric gave him a push. No luck. He went in front of the setter and started to haul him down the side of the auditorium. Luckily, the floor was waxed and the sides sloped. Rufus was forced to follow Eric.

Halfway down the hall, Rufus sat down. He was confused. What was going on? Who were all these people? What were all the smells he was smelling? And why was this boy he liked dragging him? All the way to the front row Rufus slid on his rear with people laughing at him and pointing. By the time Eric sat down in the far right seat in the front of the hall before the platform, his face was as red as Rufus's coat.

As for Rufus, he was trembling as Eric put one hand onto his back and, exerting strength, pushed him down onto his belly.

The first three rows were filled with people who had brought animals with them. Some of them held birdcages on their laps. Others had cat-carrying cases that smelled very strongly of cats. Some had little cardboard boxes with air holes punched in them set on top of their knees. Rufus didn't know what was inside, but whatever they were, they smelled very queerly and made very queer noises. He growled deep in his throat.

He was still growling when the gold-colored curtains at the front of the auditorium parted and a tall white-haired man came out. There was nothing on the platform except a strong table and a chair. The man stood behind the table.

A very tiny lady with black hair and a big Spanish

comb in it came up out of the audience and said, "Thank you for coming tonight. We are honored this evening to have the very distinguished Dr. James Reuterkrona with us. I'm sure you have all read of his remarkable mental exploits."

Rufus growled as the woman went on. Eric nudged him with his boot as she trilled, "Dr. Reuterkrona has been written up in many magazines and journals. He is the author of four books, which I am sure all of you have read. Our Society takes very great pleasure in presenting Dr. Reuterkrona tonight." She stood aside applauding. Everyone else clapped, too, except for busy people, like Eric, who were shushing and controlling struggling animals.

Dr. Reuterkrona bowed and smiled. As the lady left, he said in a soft deep voice into the microphone set on the floor in front of the table, "Thank you, ladies and gentlemen. You have been most gracious to invite me here from my home in Monrovia." His eyes ranged over the audience. "Now, who will bring up the first animal?" He chuckled as the hands of some people in the first three rows went up, including Miss Simpson's. Her hand was waving. "I will start small. Is there a fish out there?"

"Yes, there is." A tall, thin girl got up, a small fishbowl between her hands.

"Bring him up, please."

The girl passed Rufus so closely that her long skirt brushed his nose. A drop of water from the fishbowl sloshed down onto him and onto Eric.

"Oh, Lord," muttered the boy.

"What do you suppose the man will say to the goldfish?" Sandy whispered to Eric.

"What I want to know is what the fish will say to the man, Sandy."

Everyone held his breath as the girl put the bowl down onto the table and the Man from Monrovia stared down into its depths. He stared for quite a while, then he said, "Miss, is this fish off her feed? That's what she says."

"Yes, she is," cried the girl.

"My advice to you is to get a book on how to keep fish. This fish needs a tonic in her water. Then her appetite will perk up in a couple of days' time."

As the girl left, smiling, passing Rufus again in her swishing skirt, Reuterkrona called for another animal. "I'd like something small and furry this time, please."

At Rufus's sudden twitch, Eric hissed at him, "That doesn't mean you. You aren't small."

"Heck, Eric, I suppose Rufus will come just before he gets to the elephants," Sandy complained.

"Or the Saint Bernards and horses," Eric replied.

The next animal was a field mouse. According to Dr. Reuterkrona it wanted a mate. And the small boy who was its master should "be quick about it."

Now the Man from Monrovia asked for a member of the reptile kingdom. A lanky boy a little younger than Sandy came out of the row behind them. He passed close to Rufus, also. Rufus snarled and tried to rise, but Eric held him down by putting a foot on his back and pressing gently. The smell that came from the cardboard box the boy held was a very bad one in Rufus's estimation. He'd smelled it before sometimes out on the campus. Things that smelled like that lived in the ivy and jasmine bushes.

The boy stumbled going up to the platform and dropped the box, which turned on its side. Out slipped a pinkish-brown snake onto the floor of the hall. It came directly toward the right side of the front row. Miss Simpson screamed and got up onto her chair. Other people in the front row were getting up, too, including Sandy Burns, who was sighing.

She told Eric, "You get a good grip on Rufus." The dog was up scratching frantically on the floor and barking.

Sandy went to the rosy boa, picked it up, and carried it to Dr. Reuterkrona. He took it from her in both hands and held it tenderly. "Thank you, my dear," he told her. As she walked back to her seat and helped Miss Simpson down, people clapped for Sandy, who blushed.

"You done good, girl," Eric said, as the Man from Monrovia manipulated the boa and looked into its eyes. Speaking sternly to the boy owner, he said, "You are feeding him too often. Feed him less food—less often." He added, "Is his name Felix?"

The boy's jaw dropped as he nodded and took back the boa and stuffed it into its box. As he left the audience applauded again. This time the clapping was louder.

"Now," cried out Reuterkrona. "I require a cat."

A silver-haired stout lady in a pink print tent dress

was next. She waddled up to the platform carrying a cat case. She came from the left side of the hall so she didn't pass Rufus. But he watched her stomp heavily up onto the stage. Opening the case, she took out a big, fluffy calico cat. "What's its name?" she demanded. She sounded as if she didn't believe in Dr. Reuterkrona's talent.

He held up his hands to everyone. "Ladies and gentlemen, the cat and the dog are at somewhat higher levels than some other animals. My readings, therefore, on cats and dogs and pigs—if anyone should happen to have a pig with him. . . ." He paused for the laughter, then went on. "My readings for these animals will be longer and more involved. The more intelligent creatures have more to say." He turned to smile at the woman. "Your cat is not an 'it,' madam. It is a female cat. All calico cats are female."

"I know that," said the woman loudly. "Anybody who knows anything about cats knows that. What's her name?"

"Elizabeth Louisa. That's what she tells me, but that isn't what you call her."

The woman stepped back from the table. "No, I call her Betty."

"She prefers to be called Elizabeth Louisa," said Reuterkrona. He picked the cat up, held her, and tickled her under the chin. "Oh, she is really telling me things now!" he exclaimed.

"What sort of things?" asked the woman.

"That you have been married four times. That you

eat whipping cream on everything you cook. That you spend too much time on the phone and not enough time with her."

At the look on the stout woman's face, some of the people in the hall began to chuckle. The Man from Monrovia continued. "And, madam, this cat says that your present husband thinks you spend more money at the beauty parlor than you ought to, though it isn't doing you a bit of good. He thinks you put too many curls on top of your head because you believe they will make you look younger. He has complained about you to the cat, because the cat is the only person in the house who will listen to him."

"That's enough!" The lady in pink grabbed the cat from him, jammed her into the cat carrier, and locked it shut. She left the platform and *click-clicked* up the center aisle. Her silver curls bobbed above a face as pink as the flowers on her dress.

Dr. Reuterkrona waited until she was almost at the doors. Then he called out to her, "Elizabeth Louisa wants fresh milk every morning, remember! She said you let it get sour three times last week."

As the door slammed shut, people laughed and laughed. Sandy said to Eric, "Don't the animals ever say anything nice?"

"It doesn't look like it, does it?"

The Man from Monrovia wasn't laughing, only shaking his head. He came out from behind the table to ask, "Who'll bring up the next animal?"

There was silence except for the sounds of animals, including Rufus, who was growling deep in his throat. After the business with the critical cat and the angry woman, no one was eager to bring up a pet. Suddenly Eric Simpson got up. He was looking very embarrassed as he pointed at Rufus, who was standing beside him. Eric called out to Reuterkrona, "I've got a dog here with me."

"Bring him up, please."

Eric whistled to Rufus, who didn't need the whistle to start moving. But he started in the wrong direction, up the side of the hall toward the doors. He wouldn't go onto the platform, though Sandy left her seat to push him while Eric pulled him. Everyone who could see what was going on was laughing at the three of them.

Finally Reuterkrona stepped down to them. He took Rufus's head in both hands and gazed into the dog's eyes. Then the man smiled. Taking the leash from Eric, he led Rufus easily onto the platform. There he commanded, "Up." And Rufus jumped up onto the table. It was a slippery one, but the Man from Monrovia caught him just before he slid off the other side.

"Here we have a dog," said Reuterkrona into the microphone. "He has just spoken to me. He is deeply disturbed over a number of things."

Once more he looked into Rufus's eyes while Rufus looked into his. Here was a very nice man, the dog decided. He smelled of marshallow-scented pipe tobacco. He knew how to pat a dog. He was doing it now and doing it well. Rufus started to drool with contentment.

As the Man from Monrovia went on patting, he went on talking. "This dog has gone through a series of shocks. He has lost his master. He is rootless. He is lonely."

At Sandy's gasp, Reuterkrona looked down at her and smiled. "He has young friends, good friends, but they cannot give him the home he needs. I see birds near him but he does not like birds." He went on, "He does not like macaroni and cheese very much either. He wants something with a bit of garlic in it. He also wants a beef bone, a big one, to bang around and chew on. Where he is now, there are no beef bones and never will be." Now Reuterkrona fixed his eyes on Miss Simpson. "Madam," he said, "I presume you claim this Irish setter?" At her nod, he continued, "You think he might have the makings of a watchdog?"

Rufus's eyes were closed in pure delight as the man went on petting him and speaking. "This dog, madam, would run off with burglars who offered him a beef bone or even a piece of hamburger. He would let them steal himself as well as anything you owned." Suddenly his voice rang out. "This animal is an un-trammeled spirit, a free spirit, a creature of the wide open spaces. No backyard can hold him without breaking his heart. You must let him go."

"Yes, yes, I shall." Miss Simpson was standing up now, clutching at her bosom.

"Thank you, that is wisdom, dear lady." Dr. Reuterkrona bowed to her. "This dog is not for you. A Pekingese or poodle would suit you better. Darling though this animal may be to you, you must let this wild creature free."

At *the* word up went Rufus's right front paw. The Man from Monrovia understood. He took it and gravely shook it while the crowd clapped and clapped.

Miss Simpson sat down, looking a little glassy-eyed, Sandy thought. Sandy spoke to Eric. "My gosh, do you think your aunt'll volunteer to get a home for Rufus?"

"Nope." Eric was looking very gloomy. "I think you and I are stuck with him again. It's going to be up to us to untrammel him and find him a place to live." He sighed and added, as he got up to get Rufus from the beckoning Reuterkrona, "I sure wish somebody would tell my teachers that I'm a wild, free soul, too."

"No," she said hastily, "if they did, you might turn into a Mad McCormick. He's the one that got us into all this mess in the first place, remember."

7
DESPERATE
CIRCUMSTANCES

All three were looking very concerned as they walked back to Miss Simpson's house with Rufus driving ahead on the leash, trying to pull Eric's right arm out of its socket.

"He's sure strong for a dog his size," Eric told Sandy once.

"That's because he's a leader," she said, then ducked her head to avoid Eric's make-believe blow at her with his left fist.

"*Eric!*" scolded Miss Simpson.

On the sidewalk she kissed him on the cheek and told him, "I'm sorry, dear, that it didn't work out. I'm sure you'll find a good home for your dog." She took her house key out of her purse as she told him and Sandy, "I'll get poor Ali out of the bathroom now. Bathrooms are inclined to be damp, you know, and bad for the health of birds."

"Sure, we know, Aunt Fern," said Eric, sighing.

"Well, good night, my dear." And she was gone. A moment later her front door shut behind her.

"What bright ideas have you got now?" Eric asked Sandy.

"Not any really." She looked at Rufus, who was sitting on top of Eric's left foot. "I guess we'll have to take him back to my house."

"Under your house again?" Eric sounded pained. "What about your old lady and your old man?"

"I'll get around my mother."

"How are you going to do that?"

"I'll tell her how awful it was for Rufus here. Mother will understand."

"Are you going to tell her about Dr. Reuterkrona and what he said?"

"No. Remember, she thinks you and I were going to the downtown library to look up some stuff for papers we have to write at school."

"Yeah." Eric waggled his toes in his boot, but Rufus didn't move off his foot. He asked Sandy, "Do you want me to help you talk to your mother?"

"No, I don't think so." Sandy was biting her lower lip as she gazed at Rufus. "You give me his leash at my house, and you take off then. Okay?"

"If that's what you want, sure. What about your dad, Sandy?"

"If I can get around my mother, she'll get around him."

Eric sniffed. "Women!" was all he said.

She gave him a dirty look. "That's what I thought you'd say, Eric. That's what men always say when women stick together."

"Yeah, but when men stick together, women say 'men!' "

"Sure, but they don't get to say it as often." Then Sandy asked, "Eric, isn't Rufus putting your foot to sleep by sitting on it?"

"In a way, but he seems comfortable."

Sandy grabbed the setter by the collar. "Come on," she ordered, "off his foot, you oaf of a dog. Let's go back home now."

Rufus got up to look expectantly at the vanilla girl. She was taking him someplace again. Somewhere where there would be food, perhaps? He twisted his head to lick her fingers, which smelled of cheese-burgers, the dinner she had at home earlier.

Eric nudged Rufus gently with his foot. "Come on, dog. It's time for us to go back to your old neck of the woods. It looks like we've got to start all over again with you."

And so, trotting along behind the bad-smelling

motorcycle, Rufus went gagging back up Blaine Street.

Halfway there, with the cycle chugging uphill, Sandy told Eric, "You know, we could sure write interesting reports about the Man from Monrovia for our psychology class. He was lots better than going to the public library. I'll bet our psychology teacher doesn't even know there are people who can communicate with animals."

"Oh, yes, he does."

"Huh? How do you know, Eric?"

Eric said rather grimly, "We left early before Rufus got into some kind of uproar, remember? Well, you should have looked on the left side of the hall in the second row. When I was dragging the dog out, I looked over there. Our psych teacher was sitting there big as life and twice as mean-looking. The way he looks at school but even more so."

"Was he? What kind of animal did he have with him?"

"I don't know. Something else in a cardboard box. Most likely a rat or a weasel."

"Maybe so," mused Sandy. Then she asked, "Did he see us?"

"I'm sure he saw me. I had to go up in front of everybody and haul old Rufus down off the table because he didn't want to go." Eric shook his head in the round maroon-red helmet that made him look like a bowling ball riding a cycle. "I sure hope that Dr. Reuterkrona got around to interviewing what-

ever our teacher had in the box if he made a donation to get the interview."

Sandy giggled as the cycle went over a small bump
in the road. "Eric, I wonder what the psych teacher's
animal told the man from Monrovia?"

"Plenty, I bet. I'm sorry we had to miss that. Any
pet that belonged to that guy could write a whole
book. No, I think we'd better get some other ideas
for reports and really go to the library. Something
nice and safe—like the mental causes of skin rashes or
what made Mad McCormick the way he was. Or even
better, why are we doing this for McCormick's dog?
It isn't our dog. We never even saw McCormick."

"But we're so noble," said Sandy.

Eric said angrily, "Sure, we're noble and we're
nuts, too. The dog's supposed to be an untrammeled
spirit. But how about us? He's trammeled us plenty.
That dog psychiatrist gave us a pretty tall order tonight, didn't he? How many homes are there where a
dog doesn't ever have to be a watchdog and where
he can bang big bones around and eat garlic?"

Sandy put her arms tighter around Eric's waist and
clasped her hands in front of him. It wasn't easy to
do. There was a lot of Eric Simpson. "It'll have to be
a home with lots of wide, open spaces, too."

"That isn't the way I'd describe under your house,
Sandy."

Eric did as Sandy had asked. He waited only long
enough for her to get off the motorcycle and lead
Rufus away before he swung it around in the Burnses'
driveway and went *putting* off down the street.

"Come on, Rufus," ordered the girl, who pulled the setter by the collar over to the front of the house. Then she dragged him around the back of the thorn-studded pomegranate tree and tapped on the glass of one of the windows of the room she shared with Charmian. The light was still on. Charmian was up.

"Who's there?" came Charmian's voice from inside.

Sandy tapped three times—then two more.

"What's the password?" asked Charmian's voice, nearer to the window this time.

"Kiss a vegetable tonight," answered Sandy.

"That was last week's password, Sandy."

"Oh, for heavens' sake, Char, it's still me saying it. Open the window."

Charmian wound the casement window open and stuck her head out.

Rufus let out a low growl at the sight of her.

"Oh, my gosh," said Charmian. "You haven't got him back again, have you?"

"What does it look like? He got rejected by Eric's aunt. You be quiet now, Rufus. Shush up." Sandy went on, "Char, is Dad home?"

"Yes."

"What about Mother?"

"Uh-huh."

"Could you get her out into the garage to see me so that Dad doesn't know about it? Make it secret."

"What'll I tell her, Sandy?"

"Tell her anything, but get her out there alone. Okay?"

"Okay."

As Charmian closed the window and Sandy and Rufus threaded their way around the pomegranate tree again, Sandy warned the setter, "You be on your best behavior, you hear me. I have to get permission from Mother to keep you so she'll get it from Dad later on, if we're lucky."

Seated in the dark on the garage steps leading to the kitchen door, Sandy waited. She didn't have to wait very long. The clicking sound of her mother's heels came swiftly to the kitchen door. It was opened, and the garage light flicked on. There stood Mrs. Burns, white-faced and hollow-eyed, as she peered down at her daughter and Rufus.

"You're not covered all over with blood!" she whispered in a hoarse voice.

"Nope." Sandy got up with Rufus.

"Thank God. Charmian said just now that you and Eric had been in an accident, and you were bleeding all over the garage floor—though it was nothing serious." Mrs. Burns became angry. "You don't look hurt at all!"

"I'm not. We didn't have an accident."

"Was it your idea that Charmian tell me that horrible thing?" Mrs. Burns's eyes were flashing green fire.

"No, I just told her to get you outside without Dad knowing it."

"My God, Sandra, do you suppose she thought your father shouldn't be told if you'd been hurt in an accident? *That girl!*" Mrs. Burns looked at the ceiling beams of the garage while she shuddered. Suddenly she lowered her gaze to her older daughter and the dog. She demanded angrily, "Why did you want to see me out here alone?"

Sandy pointed at Rufus. "Because of him. He's back."

"So I see. What went wrong?"

"Everything. Sit down on the steps with us, and I'll tell you all about it."

Rufus sat between the vanilla girl and the woman who smelled of mint-scented hand lotion. He turned his head constantly from side to side happily sniffing the two of them while Sandy told her mother of the high fence Miss Simpson had and how Rufus howled because he was all alone there and couldn't look outside.

Mrs. Burns was patting Rufus, who was leaning on her shoulder by now. "I take it that Miss Simpson returned the setter to you when you visited her after you and Eric left the downtown library tonight?"

Sandy wished the garage light were off. She looked at her shoes as she fibbed, so her mother wouldn't see her face. "Uh-huh, we got the stuff we wanted to do papers on. It was ESP—Extra Sensory Perception, you know. The reports are for our psychology class." Her mother might be interested in hearing about Dr. Reuterkrona, but she would probably laugh if she told her. In Sandy's estimation her mother had very little imagination most of the time.

The girl went on, "Rufus howled all night there. They hate him on Lime Street now. Miss Simpson had to put her mynah bird in her bathroom because of Rufus's howling."

"What do you propose to do with this dog now, Sandra?"

"Keep him *unter das Haus* until we get a home for him." Sandy added hopefully, "He doesn't howl when he's under our house."

Mrs. Burns drew away from Rufus, who had to ooze over to keep leaning on her. "You aren't about to tell me that he likes it down there!"

"It's better than Miss Simpson's backyard. And besides we can tie him to our clothesline. That's what the Revengos did over in Canyon Crest."

Mrs. Burns got up very suddenly, making Rufus fall onto the step in the spot she had just vacated. It was warm, so he turned himself to the left and lay down on it and put his head into the vanilla girl's lap. "See, Mother, he really likes it here," said Sandy.

"Sandra, the dog might chew up my sheets on the line!"

"Oh, you can use the clothes dryer while he's here. It's only temporary. Mother, *please*! Give Eric and Char and me a chance. Give Rufus a chance. Think about him behind bars in the dog pound."

Her mother wiped the setter's red hairs off the front of her white slacks and sighed. "All right, you've played your trump card. You mentioned the dog pound. As long as the dog doesn't howl or chase our cats he can stay here—*temporarily*. But what am I to say to your father?"

Sandy lifted Rufus to his feet. "That's why I asked

Char to get you out here alone. I want you to fix it with Dad so we can keep Rufus till we find a home for him."

"That's what I was afraid you'd say." Mrs. Burns had her hands on her hips as she watched Sandy haul Rufus across the garage floor toward the outside door. "You convince me, and I am to convince your father. All right, I'll convince him, though it's going to be a struggle. Keeping that McCormick boy's dog here had better be *only temporary*, believe me. And all of this is going to cost you and Charmian something."

"What?" Sandy stopped at the outside door, looking alarmed. She stopped so fast that Rufus pulled against his collar and let out a muffled yelp of frustration.

"The dishes. Washing the dinner dishes every single night for a whole month."

"Oh, Mother." Sandy's cry was a wail of sorrow. "Pots and pans, too?"

"Pots and pans, too."

Sandy looked mournfully down at Rufus, then at her long turquoise-blue painted fingernails. "Well, okay," she told her mother. "I'll make the sacrifice for the sake of the dog. You'll do anything to get me to cut my fingernails, won't you?"

"I certainly will. Now I'm going to have a few quiet words with Charmian, who makes up such interesting stories, and then I'll tackle your father." Mrs. Burns went into the house very swiftly, surprising Sandy with her spryness for her age.

"We did it, dog!" said Sandy, as she led Rufus

around to the side of the house and began to remove the grating that covered the hole. As she pulled it away, Rufus growled deep in his throat. "Sure, I know you don't like it under there. But you've got to make sacrifices, too. I'm giving up my fingernails for you. Because of you, my mother and my typing teacher are getting what they want. Get inside, Rufus McCormick."

As Sandy pushed Rufus on the rump wishing she had Eric's muscles, she said, "You aren't to chase our cats and you aren't to howl or bark. You have to keep quiet. Okay?"

Putting the grating her father had repaired over the hole, Sandy whispered her final words of the night. "You talk too much anyhow. Boy, you really had an awful lot to tell Dr. Reuterkrona tonight. If you'd kept your big mouth shut, you might still have a home with Miss Simpson. Even her place was better than the dog pound. You'd better be grateful to us for what we're doing for you, Rufus. I just hope we can find a home for you, so you won't ever see the inside of the dog pound!"

In the days that followed, Sandy, Eric, and Charmian tried their very hardest to place Rufus in a suitable home, a phrase they'd learned from a lady on Sandy's block who knew a lot about adoption agencies. Her interest had got their hopes up, but the lady had told them quickly that she didn't want a dog.

While they worked at the problem, Rufus spent

his nights under the Burnses' house and his days tethered to Mrs. Burns's stout clothesline. He had the run of the line—twenty feet up and twenty feet back. He padded back and forth and forth and back, watching people pass on the street below the house. When he barked at children on their way to the school a block away around the corner, they sometimes climbed up on the lawn to pat him. Often neighborhood dogs stood below him on the sidewalk growling threats, but none came up to attack him when he growled back. They were all smaller than he was, and they knew the Burnses' property was "cat country." Most of the dogs had fought the Burnses' cats and knew them all too well.

Although the mockingbirds nesting in the Chinese elm tree next door sometimes dove at Rufus and scolded him constantly, they weren't his worst problem. The cats, Mary Queen of Scots and Lady Jane Grey, caused much more trouble. The two big striped cats liked to sit side by side just inside the garage, where he couldn't get at them, or lie on the hood of the car staring out dreamily at him. Sometimes they hissed at him or stuck out a gray paw abristle with long claws. At other times they did something that infuriated him most of all. One of them would sit in the garage doorway just out of his lunging reach while she washed her fur with a long tongue. When he lurched yelping at her and got caught up short by his leash, the cat would pay no attention to him at all—just go on washing.

His nights were spent waiting for morning *unter*

das Haus. He didn't howl there, thanks to Sandy's use of McCormick's words to be quiet and because of the many comforting noises overhead. Charmian somehow sensed that the noise kept Rufus quiet. She left her radio playing to keep him company while they all went out to dinner. Not one neighbor complained about Rufus. As a matter of fact, a number of people admired him for his tail-wagging friendliness and his handsome good looks.

Two ladies, one up the street and the other down the street, asked Mrs. Burns if they might walk her beautiful Irish setter. They didn't ask her twice. Both came back quite winded and happily returned the leash to her, so she could tie him to the clothesline once more. Mrs. Burns herself walked him only once. He hauled her two blocks out of her way, inspecting plants and bushes on strangers' lawns. Plunging ahead of her, both of them gasping for air, he pulled her over a field of tall grass filled with sharp buckthorn plants and finally stopped at a gopher hole.

Rufus saw Professor Burns only once for any length of time. The man come out late one Saturday night. He called very softly, "Here dog! Here dog!" When Rufus got up and put his nose against the grating, Burns removed it silently. As Rufus slid past him, the man whispered. "Go on. Run off. Show me what a free spirit you are. The paper boy's due at six in the morning. If you'd rather wait till then, hang around on the front lawn and elope with him!"

Delighted with his freedom, Rufus had spent the rest of that spring night running around the neighborhood investigating garages, knocking over garbage cans, and taking out after night-strolling cats. But at dawn he felt the call of an empty stomach.

When the paper boy arrived at six, Rufus was stretched out in the morning sunshine, sound asleep on the front porch. The paper boy, a friend of Charmian's, got off his bicycle and very quietly put the Sunday newspaper on the bottom step. Then he got back onto his bike and rode silently and swiftly away. He'd refused to take Rufus, too.

Sandy, who came out at seven in her pajamas to see what downtown movies were listed in the entertainment section of the paper, was astonished to find Rufus on the porch. She moved softly up to him and, before he woke up, got his collar in her hand. She said into his ear as he twitched awake, "You are a terrible dog, Rufus McCormick. Whoever let you out is worse than you are. I wonder who?" As Rufus got up to lick her on the ear while she squatted beside him scowling, she said, "I know. It's that nasty kid up the street. He'd better not do it again, or I'll tell Charmian to tell every girl she knows at Middle School that he's madly in love with her. That will fix him." She tugged on the collar. "Come on, dog. It's time for you to go on the clothesline."

And still in her blue pajamas, Sandy led Rufus out through the garage, found his leash on the ground next to the hole *unter das Haus,* and snapped it on, fastening him to the clothesline. She told him then, "Eric's coming over this afternoon and we'll have a council of war. You've been here entirely too long now—eating your head off, according to Dad. And he's really after us to get rid of you." Sandy glanced at the removed grating for the second time, noting how it was carefully propped up against the house, not thrown down under the clotheslines. She put her hand to her chin, thinking. Then she shook her head. She muttered to herself as she went in through the garage door, "I don't think he really would, but all the same he might. And she might, too!"

A half hour later she brought her father and mother their first cup of morning coffee. She carried the tray into their bedroom and set it down on the bureau top. As she did so, she whistled to wake them up. Lady Jane Grey and Mary Queen of Scots each gave her a sleepy green glance. Mary Queen of Scots got up, strolled across Professor Burns's stomach, and leaped down onto the bedroom rug to stretch. Lady Jane Grey didn't move. She only yawned and dug her claws into his blankets.

"Cat, don't do that!" he exploded.

"I don't know which cat you're talking about, Dad. They both always do what they just did," said Sandy. "I brought you your morning coffee."

"Huh? Coffee? It has to be the crack of dawn." Mrs. Burns brought her head up from under the blankets. But she sat up to stretch and look at her daughter. "Oh, Sandra." As she took the coffee cup Sandy offered her, she said, "Out with it. What do you want? Money for a movie? Is that why you're up so early, getting the paper? Where's Charmian?"

"She's still asleep. I don't want anything, Mother.

But you're right. I did bring the paper in already."
There wasn't any movie in town that looked worth
the money. While the coffee had perked, Sandy had
looked at the movie section.

"So you woke us up only to enjoy our company,
huh? True nobility in one so young and so early in
the morning, too," commented Burns, who came
heaving up on his pillows like a surfacing whale.

"I found something very interesting on the front
porch." Sandy watched both of her parents closely
from under her eyelashes. They were still mascaraed
midnight-blue-iridescent, because she hadn't removed the makeup from the night before. It had
smudged under her eyes making blue shadows that
gave her a fragile, abused look, she thought.

Neither of her parents noticed the blue shadows.

"What did you find on the front porch?" asked
Burns, as he reached to the bureau top for his coffee
cup. "Was it a crock of gold?" He laughed. "Or a
teen-aged dragon somebody slew just for you? Was it
some middle-of-the-night-after-your-date tribute from
Eric Simpson? Such as a recently lifted barbell for
me to pick up and dispose of?"

"No, it was Rufus."

"Oh, only that dratted dog. I'd hoped for something truly spectacular," said her father very casually,
as he held the cup and blew on the hot coffee. Lady
Jane Grey rose now to walk up onto his chest and
sniff the coffee. Then she jumped off the bed, heading for the kitchen where the cat-food bowls were
kept.

Sandy examined her recently cut fingernails, which needed more orange polish on them before Eric appeared. "I think somebody let Rufus out late last night."

"Why would anybody do that?" asked Mrs. Burns.

Burns shrugged. He yawned, then said, "Perhaps some critic of ours in the neighborhood thinks living under a house and being tied to our clothesline isn't exactly the proper life for a dog who is a free spirit."

"Well, it isn't," said Sandy, as she got up from the foot of her mother's bed. "But it's only temporary! Eric and Char and I are having a war council this afternoon. Two is the hour of truth."

"What's that? It sounds awesomely important," said her mother.

"It will be. We're comparing notes, and we're planning our combined strategy for the future—where Rufus is concerned."

Professor Burns laughed. "You ought to offer a reward to anybody who'll take Mad McCormick's mutt off our hands."

Sandy told him, with great dignity she thought, "You do not give Char or me an allowance that would allow that."

"Well said," he replied, as he took his first scalding sip of coffee. "Well said, but it won't get your allowance raised one dime. Go feed the cats; then feed that dog. Good morning, Sandra. I had hoped to sleep till ten o'clock."

As she headed for the kitchen, Sandy was still wondering about her father and mother. If one of them had let Rufus out, she didn't know which one it was. Parents worked together a lot of the time.

The splutter of Eric's motorcycle at two fifteen brought both Burns girls to the front of the house to greet him. They stood as a welcoming committee as he got off the cycle, stationed it on its kickstand, and came somberly toward them. He had a glum look on his face.

"What's new, Earache?" asked Charmian.

He grunted, "My cycle needs a new headlight."

"I mean, what's new about Rufus? Have you had any luck looking?"

Eric spread his large hands wide. "I tried everybody I know. I tried every friend my mom's got in town. The trouble is that they all know my Aunt Fern, too." He shrugged. "She's on the phone a lot. They've heard about Rufus. It wasn't as if he was somebody nobody knew anything about. They know he howls and that he's a free spirit. Some of them heard the Man from Monrovia, too. Mom's sorry she missed seeing him."

"Yeah." Sandy led the way into the dim, cool garage, where the three of them sat on the concrete floor, resting their backs against the side of the Burnses' car. While Eric put his arm around Sandy, bashing her head against the car door as he pulled her over, she said, "I put notices with our phone number on the bulletin boards at four supermarkets and ran an ad in the school paper. I even asked my typing teacher if she wanted a dog. She said, 'No, I've got three of them.' She's got a sort of ranch in Mockingbird Canyon. That's why I asked her."

"Everybody's got a dog," mourned Charmian.

"And what's left over doesn't want a dog," put in Sandy.

Charmian spoke up again. "I had a lead on a lady. She was the aunt of my Spanish teacher. I took Rufus to her house, but she and I decided that he wouldn't like it there one little bit. We decided it was more of a home for a Chihuahua dog than an Irish setter."

"What's the matter? Doesn't the aunt talk English?" asked Eric.

Charmian scoffed at him. "Earache, just because a person teaches Spanish doesn't mean that her relatives can't speak English. Sure, she can talk English. She wants a Chihuahua because of her cactus garden."

Eric groaned, "Oh boy! An Irish setter doesn't fit in, huh? A cactus garden has to have a Mexican dog. She sounds a little like my Aunt Fern, who thought Rufus clashed with her house because he was red."

Charmian shook her head vigorously, making her braids fly about and smacking her finally across one cheek. She held her hand to the cheek and said, "It isn't that. She has to have a little tiny dog. Rufus and I went into her cactus garden. It was full of things with thorns and prickles on them, and the pathways between plants aren't any bigger than this." She demonstrated with her hands. "There wasn't anyplace at all for Rufus to roam around without getting all full of cactus prickles. I mean, either his nose or his tail would get them. Guess what just sniffing a prickly pear can do to a dog's nose?"

Sandy agreed gloomily, "I know. You have to get the prickles out with tweezers. You're right, Char. The woman has to get a little dog." She turned to Eric. "Why don't we take Rufus over onto the campus and let him have a good long run this afternoon?"

"Sure, wear him out," suggested Charmian.

"Wear *us* out, too." Eric didn't sound delighted. "Maybe he'll run off."

Sandy snuggled up against him, "Oh, Eric. Maybe we'll find something about Mad McCormick."

"Now, that's good thinking, woman." Eric Simpson planted a very loud smacking kiss on Sandy's forehead. He added hopefully, "Maybe we can hand him back to Mr. McCormick in person."

"I doubt it," Charmian told him, crossing her long thin legs before her. She stared out the open garage door at the red dog, who'd come to the end of his leash and stood with his tail wagging in invitation. She suspected he was waiting for Eric to tussle with him, fuss over him, and call him "darling," so he could have his paw shaken. A moment later she added, "I think we are in very desperate circumstances."

Sandy nudged her boyfriend. "Charmian's been reading the paperback books Mother buys at the supermarket. You know, the kind with bug-eyed ladies on the cover in bathrobes running away from haunted castles. I read a couple of them. Those ladies are always in very desperate circumstances."

8

THE BEAR'S MUZZLE

Eric left his cycle parked in the Burnses' driveway and walked the half mile to the campus with Sandy beside him. Charmian had Rufus. Leashed, the setter charged ahead of her, pulling her behind him as she skated. *Whoa* meant nothing to him. In five minutes Charmian was two blocks ahead of the others.

Holding hands, Sandy and Eric strolled along after her and Rufus. "She's a good skater, isn't she?" observed Eric, as they crossed Blaine.

"She has to be. Rufus takes some pretty wild short-cuts sometimes."

They'd agreed to meet, all three and Rufus, in front of the Revengos' house in Canyon Crest. They wanted to ask about McCormick. When Sandy and her boyfriend got there, they found Charmian out in the street with Mr. Revengo, who wore a red-and-black *dashiki* today. His smallest daughter was in his arms, struggling and kicking. Rufus was cowering behind Charmian, peeking up at the child.

"Ah, Sandy," greeted the African. "I see you still have the dog?"

"We sure do."

"You decided to keep him?" Revengo sounded surprised.

"No!" cried Charmian, while Rufus tried suddenly to jerk free from her grasp on his leash.

"No," said Sandy Burns more calmly.

Just then the Revengo child kicked her father in the thigh. Her eyes fixed on Rufus, who was still trying to pull loose from Charmian, the child shrieked, "Horsie. Horsie."

Rufus yelped. Leaping forward with all of his power, he spun Charmian around on her skates and headed at a plunging run toward the campus a block away.

"Gid-di-up," Charmian's voice came floating back to Sandy, Eric, and the Revengos, as she whizzed along in the setter's wake.

"You had better go after them," advised Revengo, as he put his daughter down on her feet. She shrieked

again and started after Rufus, but she was stopped
by her father's large hands on her shoulders.

"Mr. Revengo, have you heard from McCormick?"
Sandy called over her shoulder, as she and Eric
started away.

"No, perhaps he went home to Texas."

"That figures!" shouted Eric, as Mr. Revengo
scooped up his child again.

The African started for the house with her. Shaking
his head at her, he said, "Alas, I should have told them
to seek out the kitchen lady who knows about avocados." He hugged the little girl. "But you made me
forget her, you wicked small minx."

It was downhill from the edge of Canyon Crest
graduate-student housing onto the campus. Dragged
by Rufus, who knew where he was headed—home to
the wide, open spaces—Charmian was hauled swiftly.
Too swiftly! There was a stop sign at the end of the
block. Charmian meant to obey it. Not Rufus. They
went racing past it across the road and up the steep
concrete-paved hill path. By the time Rufus had
reached the hilltop, even he was winded.

All at once he sat down to enjoy the smells, the
familiar odors of the campus bushes and trees. Caught
up short by his sudden halt, Charmian fell, tripping
over him. Winded too, she didn't even try to get up.
She was sitting with an arm around Rufus when her
sister and Eric caught up to her.

"We got here," she panted to them. She motioned
toward the wide expanse of grass on the two sides of
the paved walkway leading to the bell tower. Rufus

was standing up now, pulling his leash taut as he leaned forward into his collar.

There were people in the distance throwing Frisbees. The dog let out a strangled yelp.

Eric ordered, "Let him go, Char. He's a wild, free spirit, remember?"

"I'll do it." Sandy reached for the setter's collar and sprung the leash free.

Rufus, his tongue lolling, raced away from them toward the students. As he ran, he barked to get their attention.

"Hey, it's Rufus!" came a student's voice.

"Watch out for your Frisbees," came a second loud shout.

Rufus plunged into the midst of the Frisbee players. He ran from student to student, yelping. As the plastic saucers sailed by over his head he leaped high into the air after them, his mouth open to catch one in his teeth.

After Eric helped Charmian up, he and Sandy watched the players on the grass. While they were watching, Rufus succeeded in his own private game. A blond student with a mustache failed to catch the blue-and-yellow Frisbee. It fell lazily toward the grass beyond him. Jumping for it, Rufus caught it in midair. Holding it in his mouth, he streaked away from the group of players with the student in wild pursuit.

"He's happy now," said Sandy, as Rufus disappeared in a red flash around the corner of a building.

Charmian told her, "I hope if we have to take him home and put him *unter das Haus* again, he'll be worn out so we can push him in without any trouble. You better do it, Eric. I'm worn out already. Let's let Rufus run all over the campus first. I bet he comes back to the Frisbee game in a little while."

Eric said glumly, "If he doesn't bury the Frisbee. You know how dogs are." He pointed to the student who'd failed to catch the Frisbee and given Rufus his chance. The young man had come back around the building again, and he didn't have the Frisbee. He was grinning, though.

"Rufus got away with it," said Sandy.

Charmian laughed. "Oh, he'll be back. You wait and see."

Sandy pinched her boyfriend's arm. "Maybe Char could do as well as the Man from Monrovia if she puts her mind to it. Maybe she could go on the stage, too, reading dog minds."

"I hope she's right." Eric shook his head. "What if Rufus doesn't come back, though? What'll we do then? Remember, he knows this place a lot better than we do. We aren't students here."

"We'll wait around for him," announced Charmian. "It won't be long."

Sandy ignored her sister's words. She spoke to Eric. "We should ask about McCormick while we're here, shouldn't we?"

"Sure." As Charmian skated on ahead of the other two toward the bell tower, Eric and Sandy started toward the Frisbee players.

Two of the college students stopped their game after one of them caught the sailing saucer in a spectacular athletic jump into the sky. They looked expectantly toward the Burns girl and Eric as they came up.

Eric told Sandy, "You do the talking now. You know Mad McCormick."

"Eric! I never set eyes on him!"

"Well, your dad knows him."

"Yeah." Sandy looked sourly at Eric out of the corner of one eye. "Okay."

A tall student with a red bandanna tied across his forehead was the one she chose to ask, "Do you know somebody here named David McCormick?"

The student laughed. "Mad McCormick? Sure. Who wouldn't know him?"

"Well," Sandy said, "we've got his dog."

The other Frisbee player, a thickset dark-haired youth, nodded. "Uh-huh, we just spotted him. He's up to his old tricks, isn't he? Where's Rufus been the last few days?"

"Living at my house—temporarily," said Sandy, being wary. The students seemed to know Rufus's nature very well. Would one of them take him? She asked, "Do you know where McCormick is now?"

"Nope," said the student with the red bandanna. "I don't live in his dormitory, but that guy over there does." He pointed to a thin brown-haired, brown-bearded youth and shouted, "Hey, Bruce, somebody wants to talk to you."

Bruce came over, Frisbee in hand, to look at Sandy and Eric from behind horn-rimmed glasses. "Yes?" was all he said.

"Do you know David McCormick?" asked Eric.

"I did know him. He has gone·" Bruce was very clear-spoken.

Sandy asked, "Is he living somewhere in town?"

"No, he is not."

"Well, then, where is he?" Eric wanted to know.

"He has gone to central Texas. He will not return."

The student with the red bandanna broke into the conversation as Sandy's heart sank. "How do you know, Bruce?"

"Because Mad McCormick has written a postcard from there."

"To you?" asked Eric.

"Not to me personally. Not to anyone personally. It was addressed to the whole dormitory and was put on the bulletin board in the lobby hallway."

"Shall we go see it?" Sandy asked Eric.

Bruce told them, "There is no need to do that. It had a very short message. I read it once and memorized it."

"What did it say?" asked Sandy.

"It said, 'Good-bye forever. Remember me fondly. Somebody take care of my red dog.' "

Charmian had skated back and come over the lawn to them. She heard Bruce's words and added mournfully, "That's us."

"Oh?" Bruce looked at her with interest. "You have taken Red Rufus?"

"Not because we want to," said Sandy.

Bruce nodded wisely. "This is understandable. Rufus could be something of a trial at times."

All at once Eric asked the three Frisbee players, "Well, if you know Rufus, will one of you take him off our hands?"

The students looked at one another. The young man with the red headband said, "I can't. I'm graduating in June."

The dark-haired one said, "I've got a dog at home, and I'm going home for the summer vacation."

Bruce shook his head. "I'm going to summer school on another campus of the university." He added, "I'm sorry."

Sandy pointed to the other five players. "What about one of them taking him?"

"Except for my friend here"—and now Bruce pointed to the dark-haired student—"they are all seniors and about to graduate. This is really the Senior Frisbee Olympics. We are honored to be included as juniors to make up the right number of teams." He continued, "I am very much afraid that Rufus is still your responsibility." Now he pointed over their shoulders. "And speaking of the Unspeakable, because the Devil pops up. There he is!"

Sandy, Charmian, and Eric whirled around to see the Irish setter walking toward them. The Frisbee was still in his mouth and his tail wagging.

"Hey, Rufus, that's ours. You've had your fun," called out the boy with the blond mustache. He whistled a two-note whistle, and Rufus went to him and dropped the blue-and-yellow saucer into his waiting hand.

"Charmian Burns," Eric said, "You are a mental

marvel, too! You can really read the canine mind."
He whistled the exact same way, and Rufus came
trotting to him.

"What will you do with the dog now?" asked
Bruce, who had not gone back to his game, though
the others were throwing Frisbees once more.

"Let him run free," said Sandy.

"Excellent," Bruce said with a nod. "As I recall
he used to be particularly fond of chasing crows on
the football field."

"He doesn't like mockingbirds either," volunteered
Charmian.

Bruce agreed solemnly, "No, indeed. No four-
legged creature likes them. I've seen dogs with the
tops of their skulls bleeding, thanks to those dive-
bombing feathered fiends." Bruce smiled grimly· "I
have been attacked by them myself."

"We know. So have I," said Sandy. "And I've seen
my cats roll over on their backs and try to claw
mockingbirds out of the air. Mary Queen of Scots
does it every spring and fall."

"Does she?" Bruce looked interested. Then he said,
"Well, good-bye." He bowed slightly and marched
back with his Frisbee tucked under his arm.

"He's nice," mooned Charmian. "I wonder if he
curls his beard?"

"It's a wonder you didn't ask him!" growled Eric.
He looked down at Rufus now. "Okay, dog, you've
had your Frisbee fun. How about a little crow chasing?" He put the leash on Rufus and turned himself

and the dog around. They retraced their path to the enormous sunken expanse of grass across from the dormitories—the grass that was the football field, soccer field, archery butts, and baseball diamond combined. It was also the part of the campus where Sandy's mother and her friends hunted mushrooms sometimes. Nobody in the Burnses' household would eat them, but looking for them gave Mrs. Burns a good deal of pleasure. Her friends hadn't been poisoned yet, but her husband still refused to try them. Thinking of this, Sandy let out a sigh.

Here, on the athletic and mushroom-hunting grounds, Eric Simpson let Rufus off the leash. The three of them stood on the sidewalk above, watching him charge down the hillside through the shrubbery and onto the grass below. There was a flock of crows there all right, black specks walking in the green distance. The three watched while the dog, a streak of red bronze, came upon the birds. His excited shrill yelps floated to their ears as he raced over the lawns in the hazy afternoon sunshine.

Sandy breathed, "He *is* a wild free spirit! Wouldn't you like to do that, Eric?"

"No, I wouldn't."

"All that running ought to wear Rufus out," said Charmian, who went off to skate in circles several yards away.

Eric spoke to his girl. "We're still stuck with the dog, aren't we?"

"It looks that way."

"Oh well, the day's not over." Eric put his arm around Sandy and lifted her off her feet. "You've gained weight," he accused her.

"I know. It's because I'm eating too much. I'm worried about Rufus getting a home. When I worry, I eat."

"I know, it's easier to stuff than starve," he agreed.

They let Rufus run below them until the bells in the tower clanged out four P.M. Then Eric whistled for him. The setter came at a slower pace, a lope, up the side of the hill and onto the sidewalk. He was panting and his sides heaving, but his eyes were very bright. He stopped on the sidewalk for a moment, not looking at the Burns girls or Eric but with his muzzle high scenting the air. And then at a determined trot he crossed the street toward the central dormitory.

Eric whistled again. Sandy yelled, "Rufus, you come back here." And Charmian started out after him.

Rufus paid them no heed. He went along, moving faster once he was over the street. They followed. But the setter didn't go to the front door of the dormitory. He went into the shrubbery on the left side of the huge brick building. Eric and the girls increased their speed, but they were only just in time to see the red flicker of Rufus's tail whisking around the rear corner of the dorm.

As they reached the corner, they heard him barking. It was a brisk, small bark. And then as the three of them, Eric with the leash in hand, came around the back of the building they saw a door set behind a wall. The door was opening.

A small woman in a long white kitchen worker's coat was stepping out. They heard her cry of "Rufus!" as she bent to fling her arms around the setter's neck

"Hey"—Charmian nudged Eric—"look at that."

"Yeah, whoever she is, Rufus knows her and she likes him."

Unaware of the Burns girls and Eric, Señora Perez went on making a fuss over Rufus. She spoke to him partially in Spanish and partially in English.

"What's she saying?" Sandy asked her sister. "You're taking Spanish in school."

"Something about Davido being gone away and where have you been, Rufus?"

"I got that, too," said Eric. "She said that in English." He called out, "Hey, lady, do you know this dog?"

Señora Perez stood up, looking startled. *"Sí."* Her eyes narrowed in concern. "Who are you?"

"Friends of his." Eric pointed to Rufus.

"How did you come by him?" the woman demanded. "He is more thin. He looks poorly."

Sandy told her, "That's because Rufus hasn't got a home anymore. We're trying to find him one."

"Momento," came from Señora Perez. She went inside the kitchen and came out with a bowl of beef hash, which she set down. As Rufus devoted himself to it, she asked, "How did you come by this dog? He went to Mr. Revengo's house in Canyon Crest."

"I baby-sit for the Revengos," Sandy told her. And

she related the story of Revengo's asking her to shelter the dog and of his refusal to have Rufus back again. "We've had Rufus ever since," she finished. Then she added, "I'm Sandra Burns."

"*Burns!*" A look of dismay came over the woman's face. "The daughter of Professor Burns? That poor man!"

"Yes, ma'am, we are," said Charmian.

Eric went on while Señora Perez stared open-mouthed at Sandy and Charmian, "You seem to be friends with Rufus. Could you take him and give him a home?" He gestured toward the two girls. "I can't keep him, and they're going away soon, and besides they have cats."

"Everybody we talk to is going away," Sandy added.

Señora Perez shook her head—a gesture of deep sadness somehow, though she only shook it. Then she said in a mournful voice, "*Ay de mí*, I cannot." She asked Eric, "Were you a friend of Davido McCormick?"

"No, I never knew him. I'm not in college yet."

"So?" Her forehead was crinkled in thought. "Excuse me for another moment. I have something to show you." The kitchen screen door slammed shut behind her as Rufus gulped down the last of the hash. It had been a large bowl.

While they waited, Sandy said, "I guess we can figure that Rufus was fed here, too. He sure knew where to come to get a handout just now. This is the dormitory's main kitchen, I suppose. No wonder he looked good when we first got him. He didn't live on just pizza. I bet he got fed here every day."

Now Señora Perez was back. In her hand was a card. She gave it to Sandy. On the front was a bright-colored picture of a horse bucking off a cowboy. On the reverse were some words in block printing. Sandy read out loud, "Hang in there, señora. Something's coming up. Love. Davido."

"What does it mean?" the woman asked Sandy.

"I don't know really. We heard that McCormick sent another postcard. He said 'good-bye forever' in that one."

"*Ay de mí,*" came from the woman once again. "I understand that. I know that he was expelled for the many dreadful things he did. And I know that he will not return. What does he mean by 'Hang in there'? I do not understand those words. Perhaps my English is not so good."

Eric answered, "Your English is okay. Keep your chin up, that's what he means. Or he's saying, don't give up, something like that."

"Ah." She had a very bright smile. "What does 'Something's coming up' mean? Do you know that, too?"

"No, I don't," said Eric.

Charmian volunteered, "We know what 'love' means, though." She asked, giggling, "What did you mean when you called our dad that 'poor man'?"

Señora Perez gave a long sigh, as if she enjoyed it. "He did not like Davido McCormick."

"Well, that's true," agreed Sandy. "And Mad MacCormick sure didn't like him!"

"So much hate in the world!" mourned the woman. Then she asked, "What will you do with this poor dog?"

"Keep on looking for a good home for him," Eric answered her·

"*Bueno*. I wish you good luck!" Señora Perez patted Rufus after she picked up the bowl. "I hope you get a good home, Rufus, not too far from here so you can come visit me sometimes."

"Thank you for feeding him," Charmian told the woman, as she put Rufus, who was licking his chops, on the leash, and Eric dragged him away.

"*Adiós*," said the woman from the kitchen door. "Poor dog, poor Davido," she was saying to herself, as she went back inside. In the kitchen, while she washed her hands, she went on saying the same things in Spanish. "*Pobrecito perro. Pobre Davido.*"

Back in front of the dormitory Sandy asked Eric, "What do we do now?"

He stuck his tongue out of the corner of his mouth. "We drink! All of this exercise has made me want something to drink. In the worst way—it has."

"There are Coke machines in the basement of the building Dad lectures in," offered Sandy.

"Forget them!" Eric snorted. "I want to sit down on a chair when I drink." He pointed across the road and green sports fields. "There's a place over there that has tables and chairs on a patio. I guess it's new. I rode by it on my cycle the other day."

"Oh, there?" came from Charmian, who was nod-ding· "It *is* new. It's called The Bear's Muzzle. It's not a part of the university. It isn't on the campus."

"No, but it's just across the street from the cam-pus," said Eric. "Anyhow it's a place to sit down."

"It could cost more to drink over there," warned Charmian. "It costs less to stand up and drink than it does to sit down and do it."

"I'm rich today. I took on another lawn job last week."

"Okay, Eric. Char and I will spend your money," said Sandy.

They went as slowly as they could toward The Bear's Muzzle, though Rufus wanted to get there faster, surging ahead at the end of his tether. Finally Charmian took his leash and let him pull her along the sidewalk once more. She and Rufus were over the street off the campus before Sandy and Eric were. She was seated on one of the yellow-painted iron chairs when the others arrived. Rufus was lying down next to her with his head on his paws.

"I think maybe he's getting a little bit tired out," she told them, as they sat down, too.

"I hope so, Char," said Sandy wearily, as she and Eric sat down at the same table. Eric, who didn't care for the sun because he burned, sat under the shade of the big yellow umbrella.

The patio of The Bear's Muzzle had no other peo-ple on it, except for a short girl in a black skirt and red off-the-shoulder blouse. She was wiping off a tabletop with a sponge. Now that Eric and Sandy were seated, she called out, "Okay, are you ready to order now?"

"Yes," Charmian shouted in return.

The girl came smiling toward them. Her long brown hair was parted in the middle and put up into a clip at the nape of her neck. Her eyes were brown and her cheeks very pink under a mass of little freckles.

"Hey, it's Stephanie," said Eric all at once. He lumbered to his feet as Sandy stiffened in her chair. He looked down at his girl. "Sandy, this is Stephanie Tyler." He explained, "We took a painting course together at the museum last summer."

"Oh," came from Sandy, who was glowering.

"Sure, Eric and I and my boyfriend were in it." Stephanie's voice was a low one.

Charmian giggled and nudged Rufus with one of the front wheels of her right skate. As Eric sat down again, he asked Stephanie, "Have you got a job here?"

"In a way." She laughed. "My parents own the place. I'll be starting school here on the campus as a freshman next fall."

"What kind of place is this anyhow?" asked Charmian.

"Kind of odd, if you ask me. It's a restaurant and a pub. You know, *pub* is an English word for saloon, I guess. Well, for lunch we serve food—clam chowder and hamburgers and pizza and beer and wine. At night we have just beer and wine. The students who are old enough to buy beer come over here a lot from the dormitories."

"Can we get something to drink out here on the patio?" asked Eric.

"Sure, I'm your waitress. Lunch is over, so there isn't any food. What do you want to drink? We don't make sodas, but we've got lots of things in bottles."

Eric consulted with the girls, then gave the order. "Why is this place called The Bear's Muzzle?" he asked.

Stephanie shrugged. "Dad and Mom liked the name. It sounds sort of English—sort of like an English pub, you know. The name's crazy and the place is sort of crazy inside, too. People like it. Besides the bear's the mascot of the University of California. You know—the big football teams are called the Bruins and the Bears on other campuses."

"I know, The 'grisly golden grizzly,'" put in Charmian, nudging Rufus again with a skate wheel. This time the setter let out a yelp. She'd prodded him, not nudged in his estimation. He wriggled out of her way.

Stephanie peered past Charmian's legs at Rufus lying on the sun-warmed yellow bricks. He was a sprawl of shimmering red hide in the late afternoon glow. "Gosh, he's a beauty, isn't he?"

"He sure is." Sandy caught at Eric's hand under the table and clenched down on it.

"Is he your dog?" the Tyler girl asked Sandy.

"No, he isn't," said Eric very quickly, as he returned the pressure of Sandy's hand.

There was a long pause while Stephanie smiled down at the dog, then Eric spoke again. "He hasn't got a home, not any home at all. He used to live on the campus, but the guy who owned him got expelled, so now the dog's our problem."

"And he's almost starving to death," added Charmian, who gazed sadly at Rufus. "Well, if he doesn't find a home pretty soon, he'll either starve to death or wind up in the dog pound." She fixed her gaze on Stephanie accusingly.

Sandy looked sadly at the Tyler girl, too. She mourned aloud, "It's too bad. We've tried everyplace we could think of, but nobody wants Rufus. Poor Rufus. He's such a darling."

"Darling." Rufus caught the word. He got to his feet and lifted the right front paw to Sandy.

"My goodness!" Stephanie's round eyes grew rounder.

"Shake the paw. It's required of you," ordered Eric.

As the Tyler girl knelt and shook Rufus's sleek red paw, the Burns girls and Eric exchanged swift glances over her head. They waited hopefully, but Stephanie said nothing.

Now Eric put in, "He's a free untrammeled spirit. Like the kind of paintings you did at the museum. I remember them. They were neat."

Stephanie nodded. "That's the real me—leastwise, that's how I want to be. Free and untrammeled, too." She got up suddenly. "I'm going to bring my dad out to see him when I come back with your orders."

"Does he like dogs?" asked Charmian.

"He says he does."

When Stephanie had gone, Sandy took her comb

out of her jeans pocket· She combed Rufus along the spine, then swiftly arranged his red pelt into shining swirls. "Look beautiful," she whispered to him.

"Whatever you do, Rufus, don't bite the hand that might be going to feed you from now on," warned Eric.

"All of us should pray," said Charmian very softly to the underside of the umbrella.

Mr. Tyler was a short, heavy bald-headed man in a red, green, and white plaid shirt. He carried the tray and glasses and bottles while Stephanie came along behind him. While she poured the soft drinks, he stood over Rufus. "That's some handsome dog!" he said finally.

"Yes, sir," agreed Eric.

"He might be pedigreed," added Sandy.

Tyler asked, "Stephanie says you told her he's homeless?"

"Uh-huh," agreed Charmian, "but we've been looking after him. He likes cold pizza."

Stephanie told her father, "That's something we sometimes have a lot of, leftover from people's lunches."

The owner of The Bear's Muzzle reached down and patted Rufus on the head. "Pizza, huh?"

"He's got a nice disposition, too," came from Charmian. "We think he's a real darling."

Up came the paw on the right word. Charmian stifled a laugh. She hadn't told her sister and Eric yet, but she suspected that Rufus might have other tricks. Maybe she was a mental marvel as they'd said.

She wondered how she'd look in a purple-and-gold turban.

Mr. Tyler took the paw. He said while he shook it, "The dog seems to like me."

Eric told him, *"Dogs know!* His name is Rufus."

"Yes, they do know." Tyler asked next, "You're absolutely sure that he hasn't got an owner?"

"Absolutely sure," Eric replied. "Not anymore he hasn't."

"Well, then," the man finally said the hoped-for magical words, "he's got one now."

Eric kicked Sandy and Sandy kicked Charmian and Charmian kicked Eric under the table to express their happiness. Eric didn't show any pain in his face, though he felt his shin would be scarred for life by her skate wheels. The three of them had made a two-pronged pact as the Tylers had come over the patio toward them. They wouldn't say "Hurray!" until they were a half mile away from The Bear's Muzzle. And when they were far enough away, they wouldn't just say it. They planned to yell it.

9
"SILENCE
WILL BE OBSERVED"

Sandy and Charmian hugged Rufus, saying good-bye, and then Eric gave him three pats on the head, and they finished their drinks and left to do their "hurray."

Mr. Tyler took Rufus's leash and hauled him toward The Bear's Muzzle. "He doesn't lead very well," the man called over his shoulder to his daughter, as she picked up the glasses and bottles.

The man and dog started into a narrow entryway. At its end was a big red-and-white Stop sign. On the

other side was a poster of a circus fat lady and another
of a Hindu snake charmer. Odd smells came out of
the place as they went through the doorway. Inside
Rufus stopped to sniff, resisting Mr. Tyler's tugging
on him. He scented food, pizza, and he smelled the
sourness of beer. But there were other things—smoke
and dust and peanut-butter smells. The Bear's Muzzle
was dimly lit, but all the same Rufus found out with
the first step he took inside why he smelled peanuts.
The concrete floor under the little round tables and
chairs was totally covered with dusty peanut shells.
They were very slippery to walk upon. As he took
another step forward, Rufus slid into his new home.

"Don't worry, dog," said his new master. "Everybody does that at first. Keep your feet. You're better
off than we are. You've got four of them." He
chuckled at his own wit as he let Rufus off the leash.
"Go on, explore. Make yourself at home. There's
nobody here now; it's too late for our lunch business
and too early for night business."

As Rufus walked off carefully over the peanut
husks to sniff at the wooden walls and then meander
down a narrow, very dark hall to the other two rooms,
where the pool table and mechanical games were kept,
Stephanie rejoined her father. Holding the tray, she
asked, "Where's our new pooch, Pop?"

He chuckled again. "Exploring. Looking around.
Remember now, he can have the run of the place out
here but not in the kitchen or in the restaurant when
people are having lunch. That's against the law."

"Sure, but I think dogs are cleaner than a lot of

people I know." Stephanie put the tray on a nearby table. She tilted her head to stare up at the ceiling. She hadn't really made up her mind whether she approved of The Bear's Muzzle yet or not. Her parents got some way-out ideas at times. "I don't think I'll ever get used to this place, will you?" she asked.

"No," said her father, who looked up too. "But your mother likes it, and it *is* different. She told the decorators to make it 'different,' but sometimes I wonder how safe it is."

"I think the wires are strong enough to hold up all the junk, Dad."

The Tylers stood side by side looking at the amazing assortment of things on the ceiling—some bicycles, an old-fashioned baby carriage, a stuffed opossum, a slide trombone, three big-wheeled, red-painted farm wagons, ancient tricycles, some old hats, a surfboard, a coffee grinder, and some farm machinery from the last century, which none of the Tylers had even been able to identify. It was a marvel to them where the interior decorators had found all of the expensive old junk.

"The walls are just as wild, and this is only one room," observed Stephanie. As Rufus returned, walking with great care over the peanuts, she pointed to the bar of The Bear's Muzzle. Over it was the stuffed head of a brown bear. Flanking the bear were the stuffed heads of an elk and a bull with a ring in his nose. There were purple ribbons dangling from the bull's nose ring. Under the stuffed animal heads were pictures of ladies in bloomer-type bathing suits, oldtime ads for blood purifiers, and posters of circus performances given seventy years back. One of them had a colorful drawing of a big ape running off with a small child screaming in his arms.

"Well, it's new—even if it's old and strange. And it's making a living for us," said Mr. Tyler.

"Yes, but if something falls on my head someday, I'll let you know—if I'm still alive." Stephanie patted Rufus, who was snuffling at a peanut that was still in the shell. He had a paw on it trying to bite it open. Stephanie knelt, got it, cracked it for him, and fed it to him.

"Feed him a hard-boiled egg, too," ordered her father, who gave Rufus a pat on the rump. "Make yourself to home, old boy." And he left.

"Rufus," called Stephanie, who'd gone ahead to the bar to take an egg out of a big fishbowl of boiled eggs. While the dog waited, she peeled it. "Salt and pepper?" she asked, laughing. Then she shook her head and gave it to him. "No, it's bald. Try it."

Rufus ate the slick thing in two bites, then stared at her hoping for more. Stephanie gave him a second egg, then lifted the top off a bottle. He knew that sound. She took up a clean ashtray, filled it with something, and put it down among the peanut husks.

The setter went to it at once. He'd had this before. It was beer. In five great noisy gulps he lapped the ashtray dry. The girl said, "I guessed you were that sort of dog. You should be happy here." She stroked Rufus along the back as she poured out a little more beer for him. "We've got a long, hot summer ahead of us before I start to college. I have to work here in the kitchen, and while I do you can run across the street onto the campus. But remember, this is where you live. Okay, Rufus? Maybe when I get a day off, I'll take you to the beach with me, so we can run wild and free together on the sand." She sighed. "Boy, I wish I had red hair the color of yours, but that red color only comes in bottles of dye for people. I bet lots of people won't call you Rufus at all. They'll call you Red." She touched his collar. "Hm, you haven't got a license, have you?"

Stephanie let out a second sigh, then told the dog, "Well, you aren't going to get one either. I don't believe in licenses for dogs. People aren't fair to dogs in this country." She grabbed at Rufus's waving tail, held it fast for a moment, and then let it go when he twisted around to look at her hand. "See, you hated my holding your tail, didn't you? That was right that you did. You weren't free then. Nothing that has to have a license just to go on living in the world is a free spirit! Oh, it's okay to keep crazy car drivers off the road, but it isn't right to make dogs get licenses. If dogs have to be licensed, why shouldn't cats be licensed, too?" Stephanie lifted her arms to the wild jumbled ceiling of The Bear's Muzzle. "Why not license horses and wrens and chipmunks then? License all of the things in the zoo! And after that license the rain and the sunshine!"

Rufus sat down to stare up at her. The eggs and the beer had been tasty. Maybe more was on the way? This girl smelled of Italian spices and onions and garlic, the way someone else he'd known had smelled. It was a very pleasant smell. He yawned. All the crow-chasing had tired him. He padded over to a remote dark corner of the pub section of The Bear's Muzzle, turned around three times on top of the peanut husks, then came down on top of them, making them crackle underneath him. He didn't find them comfortable. He got up, made four more circles, and lay down again. They still crackled and crunched. Rufus gave up. There was a bench built at one end of the table. He jumped upon it, lay at full length, and at once fell asleep.

As Stephanie Tyler polished the bar preparatory to washing glass beer mugs, she said to herself after glancing over at Rufus, "I bet he gets along just fine here. He's got all the makings of a saloon dog." She looked at the ceiling again. There was an antique sewing machine suspended over her head. "I wonder why his master got expelled? I'll ask some of the students who come in here tonight. Maybe they'll know Rufus."

Stephanie, her father, and her tall, fair-haired mother learned that very night about Mad McCormick. Newcomers to the campus area, the Tylers were open-mouthed at the tales students told them of McCormick's wild pranks and how he was finally expelled.

"My goodness," Mrs. Tyler said, as she patted Rufus after they'd closed down the pub that night, "everybody seems to know you. You're a famous dog, aren't you? I guess we should be honored to have you living here."

As Mr. Tyler put mugs into the hot soapy water, he told his wife and Stephanie, "That depends. If the setter's as crazy as this McCormick seemed to be, I don't know how he's going to work out here."

"He'll work out fine," Stephanie told her father. "He behaved just great tonight. Look at him now."

Rufus was back on his bench with his head on his paws. He wasn't watching the Tylers tidy up the pub. He was asleep. Full of pizza leftover from lunch that day, three hard-boiled eggs, two sticks of dried beef, a cold hamburger patty, also leftover, a bowl of water, and a half mug of beer, he was stuffed. He'd wandered all night through the swarms of students, sniffing at their shoes and trouser legs. Some of them had greeted him with, "Hey, Rufus!" Many more had patted him and caressed him, and when he sat with his head resting on their knees as they drank beer at the tables, he'd sometimes been fed by them also. The only mishap of the night came about when a student stepped on his tail as the young man slipped on a peanut shell.

At two o'clock in the morning Mr. Tyler whistled Rufus awake and took him by the collar. "Come on, boy. It's time to go home to bed."

Startled, a sleepy Rufus was led out the front door and around the back of the big red brick building that housed The Bear's Muzzle, a bookstore, a record shop, and a bicycle shop. The Tylers walked to the apartment buildings behind. They had the entire bottom floor of one of the apartment buildings. Rufus explored the place thoroughly before he picked out his sleeping place, the large round green rug in the hallway just in front of the door, where everyone coming or going would have to step over him while he snored. And that first night the Tylers learned that Rufus was a powerful snorer!

The month of May ended happily with Rufus in his new home at The Bear's Muzzle.

He arranged his summer schedule without any trouble at all. He ate breakfast in the Tyler apartment and sometimes had a hamburger for lunch in The Bear's Muzzle, a hot one, not a leftover hamburger. His dinner was always one of leftovers, pizza and the handouts that students who came to the pub gave him. His dinner started at six o'clock and lasted till two in the morning. The rest of the time Rufus spent over on the campus, where he secretly visited Señora Perez first each morning to be given something to eat from the dormitory kitchens. Then after being petted by her he'd wander the campus. He ran away with the Frisbees that summer-school students missed catching. He chased bicycles and snapped at pants legs. He walked in and out of the dormitories when someone was entering or leaving and opened the door for him. He strolled up and down the hallways. He snoozed in doorways and on the landings of stairs.

He mooched ice cream and sandwiches from students sitting on the grass sunning themselves or studying.

And always he kept an eye out for crows or diving mockingbirds. When one of them came in sight, Rufus stopped whatever he was doing to chase joyously after them.

Though most of the summer-school people were strangers to him at first, by hot and hazy mid-August many of them knew him and called him by name. "Rufus, red Rufus," was heard everywhere.

Some nights Rufus didn't go to bed at all. He'd whine at the door of the apartment after he returned from The Bear's Muzzle, and one or the other of the Tylers would let him out—or else he slipped out past students coming inside the pub. Once more he crossed the street and headed for a very special part of the campus. The college cats came out at night around the greenhouses on the upper campus. On the cool evenings, when the moon was full, the bushes were thick with cats. In company with other campus dogs, Rufus chased cats of all sizes and sexes. The cats managed to escape his wild yelping dashes by running up trees or squeezing into tiny places he couldn't fit into. But they fled from him. And that was excitement.

He never went into Canyon Crest housing or across Blaine. The campus was his home. It was his kingdom!

And if he'd gone over Blaine he wouldn't have found Sandy or Charmian. Complaining all the way,

they'd flown to England with their parents. As for
Eric Simpson, he'd moved across town with his
mother and had a job at a malt shop six miles from
the campus.

The fall quarter began at last at the university,
and Stephanie Tyler enrolled as a freshman. Rufus
accompanied her to her first class, a lecture in English
composition. He went to sleep in the middle of it, but
he didn't snore—to her relief. In her second morning
class, though, he scratched at an imaginary flea. She
had only one more class that day. There he sprawled
across her feet while she took notes. Then he escorted
her back over the campus across the street to the
Tyler apartment.

Stephanie complimented him as she let him in the
front door and took off his leash. "You sure know
how to behave in lecture rooms. I'm proud of you,
Rufus. I don't think anyone on campus has a better
dog than I do. You're famous! Gosh, a lot of students recognize you. Because you've been so good,
I'm going to give you a candy bar. I bet I don't need
to put you on a leash at all to take you to class with
me. Tomorrow I won't use it."

That was a mistake. The next day, the second day
of classes, Rufus disgraced himself. Stephanie walked
over to the campus with him and left him outside as
she went into the office of the school newspaper to
enquire about a reporter's job. Rufus lay on the

bricks of the Commons building. He dozed for a time while Stephanie talked inside with Pamela Gould, the paper's editor.

His head on his paws, half-asleep Rufus was still aware of the many sounds and scents around him. Suddenly he jerked up his head. He'd been smelling bare feet, tennis shoes, flowering jasmine, and popcorn. But now there was another odor floating toward him on the hot breeze.

Cat! There was a cat about.

Rufus rose up. His nose led him to some bushes near the fountain in front of the Student Union building. He plunged into the shrubbery. At once a cat, a big orange-and-white one, leaped out ahead of him. She ran for the rim of the fountain and leaped from there onto one of the spouting metal fixtures. The cat yowled and clawed her way out of the fountain onto the concrete rim on the other side. From there she raced over the sidewalk onto the lawns.

Rufus landed with an enormous crash in the fountain, splashing people sitting in chairs around it. They yelled angrily at him, but he didn't pause as barking wildly he heaved himself over the far side of the fountain. Streaming water, he ran over the walk in pursuit of the cat. She was a big one and a speedy one, too! She ran, an orange blur, over the lawns in front of the bell tower and onto the walk before the huge gray library building.

Now, weaving swiftly in and out of the legs of students entering the library, she darted for one of the front doors. Rufus saw her sneak inside as an unwary girl student pulled a heavy door open. Scrabbling frantically over the brick entryway of the library, Rufus, too, was through the same door before the startled girl could pull it closed behind her. She called out "Hey" at Rufus as he charged under the nearest turnstile, which was marked "Out."

There on the ground floor of the library the dog came to a skidding, confused halt. People were stalking about—or rather people had been moving around, but all had stopped by now to stare at Rufus as he stood motionless and dripping on the polished floor.

Where was that cat? Rufus let out a wild ringing yelp. It rang from the ceiling and from every wall of the enormous ground floor. It brought a man librarian, looking very upset and stern, hurrying down toward Rufus. He started to take him by the collar and haul him outside. Rufus would have gone with him, but just then he heard interesting noises. *The cat*! She came running into the lobby from around the corner where the elevator was. Pursued by a library clerk with outstretched hands, the cat was squalling shrilly as she bounded along. Halfway toward the doors and safety, the cat spied Rufus. She sprang straight up into the air, reversed her path as she landed, and raced off out of the lobby. Her fur stood on end, and her tail was four times its size with fright. The clerk slipped as the cat darted off, but then the girl picked herself up to help the librarian, who was whistling softly and saying "Nice dog, nice dog," as he advanced upon Rufus. When the long-armed librarian made a sudden dive at Rufus, he found him gone, racing away after the cat down the slick floor.

They went, cat and dog, dashing one after the other through the building from end to end, with Rufus's toenails clacking on the bricks and tiles as he followed her westwards. At the very end of the ground floor the cat doubled back and fled east. Rufus kept her in full sight all the way, and when she discovered a dark stairway that led to the second floor and went up it, he rushed up it too.

Barking and yelping, he lurched around the second floor of the library at a dead run. The cat headed once for the elevator doors, which were open, but she wasn't fast enough. The doors closed on her before she could get through, and now Rufus was upon her! She whirled around, batted at him with a claw-filled paw, and then leaped onto his back, digging in her talons. Rufus howled in pain and sprinted away under a library table, scraping her off onto the floor.

They ran more slowly now, but still no one studying on the second floor could catch Rufus as he ran by, though several students made wild snatches at his collar. Then all at once a small out-of-the-way door was flung open. A slim, dark-haired woman, wearing a long, full skirt and high-heeled shoes, came out of it. She frowned with annoyance as she looked down to see first the cat and then a panting Rufus charging along behind the cat.

"What is going on here?" she demanded.

A girl standing on a table to keep out of the way called out, "Miss Burry, it's McCormick's dog."

"Oh, *him!*" said Miss Burry with great calm. She took off her shoes and flung them back into her office and came out into the hallway.

With long floating strides Miss Burry went down the hallway. Amazed students watched her rise up into the air and bound around the corner out of their sight. Around the corner the librarian poised herself tensely on tiptoe, her arms stretched out in front of her.

Rufus and the cat were running in circles. They would pass her soon again. Now the weary cat came staggering around the corner and found Miss Burry ready. With an ear-piercing shriek the astonished animal jumped onto a library table, ran across it, and soared as high as she could to bypass the waiting woman. But Miss Burry was prepared for that. She took three running steps forward, leaped up into the air, and gracefully caught the cat under its chest as the animal sailed toward her. Not even scratched, Miss Burry deposited the cat atop a row of books out of Rufus's reach.

Just as she did, Rufus came to a scrambling halt in the corridor. Outraged, he barked at the cat, standing spitting at him from the top of the books. Suddenly he saw Miss Burry coming toward him. He whirled around and sprinted away. She came floating after him. Now it was Rufus being chased. He ran for the stairway, and Miss Burry came leaping down in his wake. Running hard, his tongue lolling now, Rufus dashed down the reading room across the lobby and into the second reading room. Miss Burry came after him, occasionally rising high in effortless movements. She pursued the yelping setter to the far side of the building and into the encyclopedias. Before he could double back, he found her blocking his way in a narrow aisle of large books. Shaking her finger at him, Miss Burry backed him into a little room beside two librarians' desks.

Rufus was cornered in the office. The woman inside it was nearly as quick as Miss Burry. She had heard Rufus coming before she'd seen him. Ready for him and Miss Burry behind him, she had shut the door of the office. Now she shut the door they had just entered. Cornered!

The second woman, who was tall and gray-haired, asked Miss Burry, "Did you get that poor kitty, too?"

"Mercedes is safe, Mrs. Beck," moaned Miss Burry, as she sank into the other woman's chair. "She's safe on top of the *Works of Longfellow.*"

As Rufus came away from the door he was scratching at, he noticed that there was another opening in the office. It was a small one high up in the wall, a countertop. He sprang for it and reached it. But there he stayed—held fast by a strong hand on his collar. Rufus looked up, barking, into the face of the man who'd caught him, who, as it happened, was the vice-chancellor.

"Come on," the man ordered, as he hauled Rufus down off the counter. Still holding him, he called over the counter to the two women, "I've got the dog."

Miss Burry and Mrs. Beck come to the counter

together. Miss Burry asked the man, who looked a little like a beardless, blue-eyed Abraham Lincoln and who had Rufus in his stern grip, "Shall I call for someone to take the dog outside, Dr. Hopkins?"

"No, I'll do it." Dr. Hopkins grinned at her. "That was quite a show you and this dog put on just now. I heard you were a ballerina at one time. And now I believe it."

Miss Burry sighed, "I was until my ankles gave out."

"Well, no one would ever guess that they did from what I just saw." Dr. Hopkins put his hand on Rufus's back forcing him down as Rufus tried to jerk free. "Do you know who owns this dog?"

Behind the counter Miss Burry's stockinged foot gently nudged Mrs. Beck's ankle. Both women knew David McCormick and had sometimes been secretly delighted by his antics. They shook their heads at the very same moment.

The vice-chancellor pulled Rufus toward the out-side doors, holding fast to his collar. Twice along the way he asked passing students if they knew who owned the Irish setter.

One of them truly didn't know. The other *said* he didn't. He knew that Dr. Hopkins was new to the campus. He knew that if he hadn't been new, he wouldn't have to ask about Mad McCormick's dog. And Hopkins might learn that Rufus belonged to the nice people who owned The Bear's Muzzle.

Outside the library Dr. Hopkins asked the same

question of incoming students. No one knew who the red dog's owner was. No one at all.

Finally the vice-chancellor turned Rufus around to face the library. He told him, "Don't go in there again, you nobody's dog, you. Even if you can't read, you ought to know that there's a sign on the front door that says *No Dogs Allowed."* He laughed. "That goes for cats, too. There's another sign that says *Silence Will Be Observed.* I guess I'll let Miss Burry dispose of the cat." He gave Rufus a pat on the rear, then released his grip on the setter's collar, and stood watching as Rufus went at a brisk trot down the library entryway and turned right toward the dormitories. It was time to visit Señora Perez and get some breakfast.

Hopkins watched him go. "That animal didn't have a license," he said to himself. "He looks too well-fed to be a stray. I imagine he belongs to some student, and the kids I've asked about him are covering up for his owner." Hopkins sighed, thinking of his own days as a college student when he'd been so poor that he took any job available just to keep on eating and going to school. "Well, I'm glad I let him go so he can have the run of the campus a little while longer before the police start rounding up the dogs."

Clasping his hands behind his back, Dr. Hopkins started for his office in the Administration Building. As he walked along, he thought of the news he'd had that morning. The regents of the University were coming again before the middle of October, next

month. He hadn't been at this school to see them
arrive, but he'd heard what went on before they came.
He'd also heard that many students didn't like the
campus preparations for the regents.

"Lord," Hopkins muttered to himself, "green
smoke and a rubber chicken in the governor's lap.
That was certainly a wild tale Professor Burns told me
over lunch yesterday in the Faculty Club. He said
that the chicken was meant to land on him, not the
governor, but who knows what that demented boy
truly had in mind?"

Rufus came to the rear door of The Bear's Muzzle
that afternoon and barked to be let in after some
more hours of exploring the campus and chasing
birds that got away. Stephanie, who held a long-
handled rake, let him in and stood over him sighing.
"Oh, dog, have you ever been bad today! Seven people at least came up and told me what you did in the
library." She laughed. "You know what? You're going to be in the school paper because of what you
did. And I'm going to get to interview the librarian
who used to be a ballet dancer. I'd sure love to be a
ballerina!"

Practicing a ballet step, Stephanie balanced on one
foot and stuck her other leg straight out behind her.
Mrs. Tyler came in and took in Rufus and her daughter's posing in one quick angry glance. She said, as
she took up the rake Stephanie had put down to be
a ballerina, "I had a phone call earlier today, Stephanie. It was about Rufus."

"Oh?" Stephanie lowered her leg.

"Yes. Oh! It was a friend of mine who works in the library. It seems that Rufus created a lot of trouble in there this morning."

"All Rufus did was chase a cat around for a little while. That was a natural thing for a dog to do."

Mrs. Tyler paused leaning on the rake. "The vice-chancellor had to take him outside, I hear." Now she began to rake peanut shells over the floor, spreading them evenly. "That's not so good, Stephanie. We want to keep on good terms with the people in charge on the campus. This dog belonged to that McCormick boy, remember? That seems to be enough to give Rufus a bad name."

"Oh, Mother! Dogs don't have to worry about their reputations."

Mrs. Tyler suddenly thrust the rake at Stephanie. "Well, I happen to think that they do, and so does your father! Not everyone was amused by what he did today. Some faculty members who were doing research in the library complained about the terrible ruckus. We want you to find a new home for Rufus."

"But, Mother!" Stephanie wailed.

"But me no buts. Start working right this minute on getting him another owner. Find a home for him. That's absolutely final, Stephanie." And Mrs. Tyler left swiftly.

Stephanie looked down at Rufus, who was sniffing hopefully at the closed kitchen door. "Did you hear that, dog? You've got to go!"

* * *

She learned in the next ten days that no one she knew wanted Rufus, no matter how hard she tried to place him in a new environment, as she put it to herself. She made posters, which she taped to the outside arches of the library, and she ran an ad in the campus paper that said, "Red dog, red dog, take him. He's free." It listed Stephanie's apartment phone number.

But no one came forward in the first days of October to ask her for Rufus as she took him to class with her on the green plastic leash she'd bought to match his collar.

One afternoon, while Stephanie was at her desk in her room with her bare feet on top of it and a big book in both hands, her phone rang. A home for Rufus? Putting the book down she stepped over the setter, who was twisted around on a rug biting at a nonexistent flea on his rump.

It wasn't a home. It was Pamela Gould, the editor of the college paper, a friend of Stephanie's. Stephanie admired her greatly. Pamela was a senior and very important on campus. Her voice was crisp as always, but there was a note of great excitement in it. "Stephanie, I've had the word today."

"What word?"

"The word from heaven. The gods are returning to earth!"

"Huh?" Stephanie, who was often puzzled by Pamela, looked through her open bedroom door at Rufus, who was now trying to bite his back inasmuch as he figured the flea had moved north along his spine.

"Stephanie, I'm telling you about the regents. Re-

member, I told you about them last week. And about
what David McCormick did last spring. Well, the
regents are coming here again. I had it from a friend
who works as student help in the office of the vice-
chancellor. I'm calling you about Rufus." Pamela
snorted, then said, "Drat that dog!" Now she went on
speaking very swiftly, telling Stephanie more about
the regents and then about the dog roundup and after
that the dog-pound jail. She finished with, "Would
your parents let you rescue Rufus from the pound if
he got caught by the campus police?"

"No, the way they act you'd think he was Jesse
James."

"Okay. When you see the school getting its face
scrubbed, you'll know the regents are just around the
corner. That's the time to tie Rufus up. Keep him
off the campus." Pamela laughed into the phone.
"Watch for something else too. Wait until you see
what some of the students are planning to do when
that time comes!"

Without waiting for Stephanie to ask her what,
Pamela hung up. Stephanie spoke to Rufus, who'd
given up on the flea and who'd ambled over to her,
wagging his red plume of a tail. "What am I going to
do with you? My folks are sick of the sight of you.
And now I'm supposed to tie you up because the
regents are coming here. I think you should have
been named Trouble, not Rufus."

10
THE ELEVENTH REGENT

Stephanie kept close watch each day she went to classes with Rufus leashed beside her. Three days after her talk with Pamela over the phone she noticed that the college groundsmen, the gardeners and others, were busier than usual. There were window washers on platforms, polishing the high windows of the classroom buildings and dormitories. The arches in front of the library and under the Humanities Building were being cleaned with hoses, and the student writing on them scrubbed away with stiff brushes. Her poster offering Rufus had been torn down. The sprinkler systems were going like mad in the shrubbery and on the lawns. No one could loll on the grass anymore because of them. The fountain in front of the Student Union had been turned off and was being cleaned out inside. Men were trimming bushes all over the place. The walkways were being swept clear everywhere she and Rufus went. Much of the time they had to detour around the hosing-down that followed the sweeping. The big rug that belonged in the Student Union, the place where students gathered, was packed up and lugged to the Faculty Club for the regents.

It was worse than spring housecleaning! It dismayed Stephanie and it dismayed others on the campus. Everyone felt that the whole school was being turned upside down—and too soon again. Professors got more snappish when students went to see them in their offices asking about their grades on examinations. The secretaries and library people seldom smiled anymore. And the students were very angry that their rug had been taken away.

The campus cleanup was still going on one Monday morning in the middle of October when to the Tylers' annoyance their apartment phone rang at seven A.M. Stephanie lurched to answer it in her pajamas and instead of saying "Hello," as she meant to, came out with one word, a sleepy half-sneezing "Ho."

"Ho, ho, yourself!" Pamela Gould's voice rang very clear and far too loud. "Tie Rufus up today.

The dog roundup has begun. It started late yesterday afternoon after you and Rufus had left the campus. The police are out hunting right now. I saw them get a cocker spaniel in the syringa bushes just five minutes ago when I looked out my dorm window."

By now Stephanie was wide awake shouting into the receiver in a panic. "Rufus isn't home. We let him out last night. Hang on. Wait a minute. Let me go see if he's come back." She went to the front door, opened it, and looked out. There was no Rufus lying on the Welcome mat. Stephanie whistled. No auburn streak came running to her to be fed his breakfast. She hurried back to the phone. "Oh, Pam, maybe they got Rufus, too?"

"Well, maybe not. He's pretty fast on his feet. Good luck, Steph. If I see Rufus before you do, I'll hide him until you can come get him." And Pamela hung up because someone else was standing behind her waiting to use the dormitory phone.

Ten anxious minutes later Stephanie heard a series of wild yappings from outside. She went to the door again and delightedly opened it to the Irish setter, who plunged inside past her. She saw that his tongue was hanging out and that he was panting. So she guessed that the campus police had been after him. And so they had. He'd made it over the street to safety only a couple of feet ahead of two winded policemen.

"You'd better be careful," she said. "The regents are coming!"

The next day they arrived. There were eleven of

them this time around, but the governor was not with them. From the patio of The Bear's Muzzle Stephanie saw them touring the campus escorted by other people. Yes, it was the moment to tie Rufus up! She had an eight o'clock class and she wasn't going to take Rufus to it, even on his leash.

She went back to the apartment, shook Rufus, who was still sound asleep on his favorite rug, awake, and put him on the leash. She hauled him into the kitchen where her mother was sitting in her bathrobe reading the *Enterprise,* frowning at the news of the world.

"Mother, the regents are here now. I'll lock Rufus in the storeroom if that's okay with you?"

Mrs. Tyler looked up and nodded. "All right. If we lock him up here in the apartment, he might tear the place to bits." She waved Stephanie and Rufus away as she took a pink curler out of her hair and sighed at the news on page two.

Stephanie dragged Rufus to the little storeroom behind The Bear's Muzzle. She unlocked it and pushed Rufus inside among the barrels, boxes, and empty soft drink cartons and peanut rakes. As she shut the door on him, she called through a crack, "It's for your own good, dog."

Rufus sat down in the dark. No people near him. Nothing but Stephanie's retreating footsteps. No food. No music anywhere. He lifted his muzzle to the black ceiling and let out his first howl of the morning. He howled from eight A.M. to twelve noon —"without drawing a breath," according to Mrs. Tyler. Every time he let out a new howl she grew

more nervous. She had an entire women's club coming to The Bear's Muzzle for lunch at twelve thirty.
They were important customers, and she wanted them
to like the place and come back. It wasn't every day
that thirty-five ladies came to eat hamburgers and
clam chowder.

At twelve fifteen Mrs. Tyler went to the storeroom
and opened the door. Rufus came leaping past her
so fast that she had to jump out of his way. She'd
hoped to take off his leash, but he hurtled out of sight
too swiftly for that. She said aloud as she saw his tail
whisking around the corner of the building, "Oh
dear, I hope I haven't got Stephanie in trouble by
letting him go. But my nerves can't take that animal's
noise a moment longer. He was driving me mad!"

Rufus went quickly, trailing his green leash behind
him across the street and onto the campus. He was
free again. The moment he was through the parking
lot and onto the grass he heard the sounds. People!
Up went his head. It was the kind of noise a lot of
people made. Crowds were full of interesting odors
and very often where there was a crowd there was
food. More than that, there were always legs moving
about. Dogs like the excitement of being in the center
of people milling around.

He began to gallop toward the bell tower. That's
where the people were. The bell tower was the assembly spot for everyone when something was happening. Today's event was what the students had
been planning for days.

There were twenty-three students there in a body.

Stephanie and tiny, blue-eyed Pamela Gould were among them. These two girls carried note pads and pencils because they were reporters, but some of the other students carried signs nailed to pieces of wood. They were there to protest—peacefully but all the same protesting.

All of the signs were homemade, painted on cardboard cut from boxes. And each sign was different.

A girl student with long black bangs half covering her eyes carried a sign printed in Old English style letters in blue and gold, the colors of the University of California. It read:

**O Dearly Beloved Regents,
Please Don't Come Calling Here
More Than Once a Year**

The fat girl standing next to her had a plainer one done in red paint that said only:

Abolish Tuition

The very tall young man who was behind her carried a sign that stated:

**Share the Wealth
Make Students Rich Too**

Another male student, a much shorter one, was leaning against the side of the bell tower with a large sign that read:

**Fire All of the Professors
Let's Start All Over Again**

It was also in Old English lettering because the young man was the black-haired girl's boyfriend, and she liked to do Old English lettering.

The long-haired blond girl, who sat out on the grass at a distance and who was eating a breakfast bun, had propped her black-painted sign up against her shoulder. It said:

**Down With The Automobile
Bring Back the Horse and Buggy**

Another sign was painted in green. A thin boy with medium-length curling brown hair held it very high above his head. On it was a badly spelled:

Steak Two Times a Weak in the Dormituries

A young man Stephanie had often served hamburgers to in The Bear's Muzzle lugged a huge sign in big block letters that stated in bright blue:

**Give Us Back Our Fuzzy Rug, O Regents,
and
Let Us Buy Beer in Our Student Union**

There were other people below the bell tower besides the students, Stephanie, and Pamela. There were quite a few faculty members, the dean, vice-chancellor, and the chancellor, and all eleven regents. The dean, vice-chancellor, and chancellor were all dressed in dark blue suits. So were ten of the regents, who, to Stephanie's way of thinking, were all old men with gray hair and eyeglasses.

The eleventh regent was different. For one thing this regent was a "she."

She was a small thin lady in a bright-yellow dress and a big floppy strange-looking white hat. It had strings all over its top—to Stephanie's mind it looked a lot like a plate of spaghetti without the tomato sauce on top. And the lady was trying her best to defend her hat from diving mockingbirds.

She wasn't paying much attention to the student protesters. While the other regents and the college people looked at the signs and smiled, the woman was staring toward the safety of a little tree a small distance from the bell tower. She seemed to figure that the birds couldn't get at her hat if she stood close under a limb. Stephanie suspected that, like most Southern California people, she knew all about mockingbirds. They had no respect for man or beast. Stephanie was grinning at the sight of the woman scampering for the tree to save her hat from being attacked by mockingbird beaks, when all at once Pamela caught her by the arm, knocking her pencil onto the grass.

My God, *look*!" she hissed into Stephanie's ear.

"Oh, no, he's *loose*. Somebody let him out!"

Stephanie wailed softly as she spotted Rufus bounding toward her. She looked on in horror, wishing she could stop him somehow.

And then for an instant he did stop. He'd become aware of something exciting happening nearby. Someone was running *away* from the crowd. Someone to chase? Someone who might play? Now to the setter's ears came the loud scolding squawk of mockingbirds. Mockingbirds! The growl started deep in Rufus's red chest. Something to chase. Frisbees and birds? What better thing than a feathered Frisbee?

He changed his course for Stephanie to that of the lady regent. He plunged through the crowd toward her just as one of the gray-and-white birds came streaking toward the top of her hat again. Rufus tried to leap into the air beside her to drive off the bird. But as he leaped, the student who carried the sign about steak in the dormitories stepped backwards out of the dean's way when the dean gave him a dirty look. His sign hit Rufus hard on the shoulder as the dog sprang up. Pushed off balance by the sign, Rufus fell. He fell against an elderly man next to the student. The man, a regent, plopped to the ground as Rufus scrambled up and prepared to go for the next mockingbird that came swooping down.

The woman regent was hurrying for the library holding her hat onto her head. She'd given up trying to reach the tree. Rufus tried to go after her but could not. As he'd heaved himself up, two things happened. A large-footed professor stepped on the end of the leash while the dean grabbed hold of his collar.

Rufus lay on the ground, held down by both men, while the old regent was helped up by the chancellor, who was close by.

"Are you all right, sir?" he asked the regent.

"I think so," said the regent, sounding shaken. He'd landed sprawling half on grass, half on concrete.

Now the chancellor pointed at Rufus. "Who owns that red animal?" he demanded of everyone present.

The professor, who was still standing on Rufus's leash, answered, "I believe he used to belong to a student who was expelled last year."

"What student, Dr. Burns?" asked the furious chancellor, as the injured regent was very tenderly led by some professors to a folding chair set just under the bell tower.

"The student with the rubber chicken," replied Sandy's and Charmian's father, who was feeling very foolish at the moment. He stepped off the leash. The dean had a good grip on the Irish setter by now.

"McCormick!" fumed the chancellor. "Well, he's gone. Who owns this animal at the moment?" he asked Burns again.

"I have no idea," said Professor Burns. And that was true enough. His daughters had said only that they'd found a home for the dog last spring. When they had tried to tell him where, he had said that he wasn't interested as long as the "doggone dog was gone." Now he was glad that he didn't know. The look in the chancellor's brown eyes was very chilly indeed.

"All right," snapped the chancellor to the dean and Dr. Burns. "Hold onto the dog until the campus police arrive." He looked around at the students. "Now you see why I have the dogs rounded up here, don't you? They're a menace to life and limb sometimes."

There was a silence while a professor went to call the campus police.

Stephanie whispered to Pamela. "Should I tell them that I own Rufus?"

"No, don't do that," advised the editor. "It could get you into big trouble if you did. Keep quiet."

Troubled, Stephanie looked on as Rufus was grabbed by two campus policemen when the dean released him. The two girls were still side by side as Rufus was pulled past them, trying to slide his head out of his collar. But one of the policemen had tucked his fingers under the collar, and the other had him by the leash.

The lady regent was standing on the library steps by now. She waited there until the other regents, including the limping one Rufus had hit, joined her along with the college people. They all went inside together. Now only the students and the campus police and Rufus were left behind under the bell tower.

The students booed and hissed as the police took Rufus away to their parked car on the broad sidewalk, where no other cars were permitted to go. The college police headquarters was way out near Blaine Street —away from other buildings. Still struggling, Rufus was dragged out of the white police car and into the fenced yard behind the headquarters. There his leash was removed and he was tied fast by a rope to the trunk of a tree. Then the police walked off and left him.

Alone! Totally alone! Rufus did what he always did when there was no one at all about. He howled to the green leaves over his head. He went on howling until one of the policemen walked out with a bowl of water and set it down.

He told Rufus grimly, "Okay, dog. You can howl all night if you want to. I go off duty at five o'clock, so I won't have to hear you. I called the dog pound. They're going to send their truck out after you around eleven o'clock tomorrow morning. And then you can howl out there at the pound—for as long as they let you."

Rufus howled while Stephanie pleaded with her parents without success, and Dr. Burns kept silent at home about the setter's being in the hands of the campus police. He valued peace and quiet in his house. He had kept quiet about the great cat and dog chase in the library also, though he rather regretted having missed it.

Stephanie learned where the regents were staying. She called the motel near the campus and heard that the regent Rufus had knocked down wasn't sick. He'd even gone out to dinner with the others. Then she went over to the newspaper office to consult with Pamela.

She found the editor very busy with two other students. One was the girl with black bangs. The other was the curly-headed boy whose sign had hit Rufus. All three had paintbrushes in their hands and were down on their knees on the floor near two cans of paint. They had taken the signs used that morning off their sticks and had turned them over to paint on their backs.

"Don't just stand there. Grab a brush and help us out," Pamela ordered Stephanie.

Stephanie read two finished signs first. "Hey, all right!" she said. "Those are neat."

"We think so too," said Pamela, as she looked at the black-haired girl's elegant sign, which was again done in Old English lettering.

The next day while Rufus snored past daybreak because he'd worn out his lungs from howling, the students put on their second protest. They lurked under the bell tower for the regents to appear down the sidewalk on their way to tour the Chemistry Building. This time when they, the chancellor, vice-chancellor, dean, and escorting faculty came in sight, eight sign-carrying students moved in on them.

Four of the signs carried the words:

Liberate Rufus, Everybody's Dog!

Every word in it was red except for *Everybody's,* which was in black.

The other four signs stated in Old English lettering:

Free Rufus, Nobody's Dog!

All of the words on it were black except for *Rufus,* which was red.

The students lined the walkway on each side as the regents went by. No one smiled or nodded at them, and the chancellor looked less than pleased. The vice-chancellor seemed mournful, and as for the dean, he was wearing dark glasses. The old regent who had been knocked down was with them and not even hobbling.

Stephanie poked Pamela in the ribs. "He's okay. But Rufus is locked up because of him. It isn't fair."

The woman regent who had had trouble with her hat yesterday came walking along with the dean of women last of all. The two women were deep in conversation.

Today the lady regent wore a floppy blue hat and a blue-and-white checked pantsuit. She noticed the signs. She stopped, putting her hand on the arm of the dean of women. They talked together for a moment. Then the little woman regent walked straight up to Stephanie and Pamela.

She had a ringing voice and very bright blue eyes.

"What's this all about?" she asked, waving her hand at the signs.

Speechless with fright, Stephanie left the talking to Pamela, who was more experienced at it. Pamela

spoke calmly, though Stephanie saw how her hand
tightened on the sign she was carrying. "Ma'am, it's
about the Irish setter who saved you yesterday from
the mockingbirds. The birds must have thought your
hat was made out of white worms."

"*Worms?*" The little woman was startled. She
laughed. "Well, perhaps it did look like that to a
bird. I've had wasps and bees attack me when I wear
a flower perfume or a bright-colored blouse." She
shrugged her shoulders. "I bought that hat in Italy
because it reminded me of spaghetti. Who knows what
a mockingbird is thinking?" She smiled at the dean
of women, who'd come up beside her.

Then she asked Pamela, "What about the dog?
Do the signs refer to him?"

Stephanie found her voice. She said, "Yes, ma'am,
they do. He needs liberating in the worst way. The
campus police have him. He's going to the dog pound.
I called the police this morning and they told me."

Pamela looked at her watch and frowned. "In half
an hour he'll be on his way."

The man student with curling brown hair added,
"That's usually a one-way trip for dogs, you know."

The dean of women sniffed but said nothing. She
looked away from the signs to the top of the bell
tower.

"Rufus was a free spirit," put in Pamela eyeing
the woman regent.

"Yes, I believe he was," she agreed. "I saw him
chasing toward us yesterday as I was leaving. He was
a beautiful dashing sight."

"Not anymore," came from the girl with black bangs.

"Mrs. O'Connell, we'd better catch up with the others," prompted the dean of women. She nodded toward the men, who were turning in a group onto another walkway by now.

But the lady regent didn't go. "The dog pound, you say?" She was tapping her teeth with a silver-painted fingernail as she spoke. She sighed. "I had to take a dog there when I was ten years old. I have never forgotten that." Suddenly she turned to Stephanie. "How far is it from here to the police, my dear?"

"Half a mile maybe," answered Pamela, who then went on, "I'm the editor of the school paper. Gosh, it would make a great story for us if you could liberate Rufus McCormick."

Mrs. O'Connell had a large laugh for someone as small as she was. "An Irish setter with an Irish last name!" She looked about her. "How do you suggest we get over there before the Humane Society does?"

By this time more students had gathered to listen to the conversation, and the regents, officials, and faculty were out of sight.

"How about bicycles?" asked one of the newcomers. He gestured toward the long line of bike racks in front of the library.

"Oh, no," said Mrs. O'Connell. "I haven't been on a bicycle for forty-two years."

"Well, go with Dr. Parman then." Pamela gestured toward a youngish man with bicycle clips around his trouser legs. He was just getting off a bicycle-built-for-two with another young man.

"Good heavens," came from Mrs. O'Connell. "I've never been on one of those at all!"

"Nothing to worry about with them," said Pamela. "The person up front does all the steering. All you have to do is pedal." She called out, "Dr. Parman!" as the professor parked his double bike and the other rider hurried up the steps onto the library walk and inside.

The professor came toward them. He had yellow hair, brown eyebrows, and a beard that verged on yellow-orange. He asked, "Does somebody want to see me?"

"This is Mrs. O'Connell," Pamela explained before the dean of women could get a word in. "Mrs. O'Connell needs transportation to the campus-police building." She added, "She's a regent!"

Professor Parman's eyebrows shot up to his hairline. He said nothing, but his sweeping glance took in the students' signs.

"How about taking Mrs. O'Connell with you?" asked Pamela.

He still said nothing, but he jerked his thumb in wonder toward his double bicycle.

Pamela nodded. "Yes, on that."

The young professor looked at the lady regent questioningly.

She shrugged and headed toward the bike racks as the dean of women called after her, "Mrs. O'Connell!"

"Stephanie, you take my bike," whispered Pamela. "It's the green ten-speed third from the left. It isn't locked."

Stephanie handed her sign over to Pamela, took a deep breath, and went to the green bike. As a dazed-looking Dr. Parman got his bicycle out of the rack and helped Mrs. O'Connell onto the rear seat, Stephanie straddled Pamela's bike, praying that she wouldn't fall off or run into Parman's. She hadn't ridden a bicycle for two years—not since she'd learned to drive, and besides she'd never been so nervous in her life.

They started off with the bicycle-built-for-two in the lead, then Stephanie wobbling along, and after her came six others as an escort of honor. As Mrs. O'Connell and Professor Parman glided past the bell tower, Pamela snapped a picture of her for the paper. She smiled as she watched them go off down the wide walkways. She'd picked her professor with great good luck. Dr. Parman taught mathematics. Math professors were either stuffy or a bit wacky, she'd discovered in four years at this school. Dr. Parman wasn't one bit stuffy.

The dean of women stared after Mrs. O'Connell and the others for a long moment, then she turned about and almost ran toward the Chemistry Building.

Stephanie and the others heard Rufus before they saw him. He'd been awakened by the policeman who'd brought out a bowl of dog food for him while Stephanie and Pamela talked with the regent. The policeman had felt sorry for the dog that was on his way to the pound and had bought the food for him out of his own pocket. Now that he'd eaten and regained some of his strength, Rufus had begun howling again.

He stopped the moment he spied the bicycle parade. People. Lots of them, and on bicycles too! He came to the end of his tether and strained forward as they rode into the yard that surrounded the police headquarters.

"Rufus!" cried Stephanie, who got off Pamela's bike and let it fall to the ground because Pamela claimed the kickstand didn't work. She came rushing up to Rufus and threw her arms around his neck. He was still there! They were in time!

Mrs. O'Connell came up next, breathing a bit heavily, and with very pink cheeks. Dr. Parman stood behind her looking mystified.

"This is Rufus McCormick, Mrs. O'Connell," Stephanie said very clearly. And very cleverly she added, "Isn't he a darling, though?"

At the special word Rufus raised his paw. Mrs. O'Connell stooped a little, took it, shook it, then let it go. "He is a very nice dog," she agreed.

Rufus sniffed at her hand. She wore a perfume from France that cost seventy dollars for a tiny bottle, but to his nose she smelled like gumdrop candy. He liked gumdrops, even if they did stick in his teeth. He rose up now on his hind legs, put his paws on her shoulders, and licked the side of her face and neck. The perfume, like all perfumes, didn't taste as good as it smelled.

Stephanie told the lady regent, "Rufus *knows!*"
That worked with dog people and she suspected Mrs.
O'Connell was a dog person.

But to her horror the woman gave her a stern look
as Rufus dropped down. "Yes, I use that phrase
myself, my dear. Come on now, who really owns this
dog? He has a collar, I see."

"All right, ma'am." Stephanie told her the tale of
the library and of her parents' demand to find a new
home for the setter.

While Mrs. O'Connell was looking down at Rufus,
who was looking up at her, the girl mourned, "Well,
I can't find anybody who'll have him. I suppose if
nobody'll take him and he has to be carted off to
the dog pound this morning, he's as good as a dead
dog right this minute."

Up went the setter's red satin ears! He had just
heard *darling* and now this girl who'd been feeding
him for a while had said "dead dog."

Rufus performed his second trick on cue. He
flopped down onto his belly, rolled over, closed his
eyes, and stuck all four feet beseechingly into the air.

"Dear heaven," said Mrs. O'Connell. "He is
trained, isn't he?" She glanced at Stephanie again.
"Or are you coaching him to do this? I caught that
bit about *darling* too, you know."

"No, ma'am, I didn't know about this." Stephanie
and the others were all staring at Rufus, who was still
playing dead. She asked Mrs. O'Connell, "How do
you suppose we get him to stop doing that? It gives
me the shivers."

"I think I know," Dr. Parman suggested. He stepped forward and snapped his fingers.

Up sprang Rufus.

Mrs. O'Connell tilted her head to measure the professor's height. "Young man, how did you know what to do just now?"

"I used to have dogs when I was young."

"You're still young," she told him. She added, "Why don't you endear yourself to the students here and give the dog a home?"

"Well, I . . . ." He hesitated.

"Have you got a wife who would object?"

"Not yet."

She sniffed. "That's what I thought," she told him, as she eyed his shabby green tweed jacket, red shirt, yellow socks, and blue trousers. "Where do you live?"

He pointed toward Blaine Street. "Over there in an apartment."

"Do they allow pets?"

"I don't know." He shook his head. "I never asked if they did or not."

"Don't ask," said the regent. "Smuggle the dog inside until you can find a good home for him."

Too stunned to say no, the mathematics professor only nodded as he stared at Rufus.

"Now!" Mrs. O'Connell pointed at three campus policemen who had come out of the building to stand watching and listening. They had not smiled when Rufus played dead dog. Still, it didn't really please them to have to ship the campus strays off to the pound either.

"You, sir!" The lady regent's stabbing finger picked out the largest of the policemen. "Release this animal. He is no longer nobody's dog. He has a home. He is a faculty dog! And you—go get his leash, please." She pointed to the smallest policeman, who hurried toward the building after the leash.

When Rufus's rope was taken off, she patted his neck saying, "As of now, you are liberated." When his leash was snapped to his collar, she spoke to Dr. Parman. "Please lead him back onto the campus."

"Um-m," was all the professor said.

Mrs. O'Connell held out her arms to the third policeman, who set her on the back seat of the big bicycle. Moments later they were off, heading east toward the bell tower. As they circled out beyond the police station, they passed a white van coming in. It had *Humane Society* painted on its sides.

"Hooray!" shouted Stephanie, as she pedaled behind the bicycle-built-for-two. Five of the other cyclists bringing up the rear hissed at the van. The sixth stuck out his tongue as he pedaled past it.

That same afternoon Dr. Parman took Rufus in his very small car to the veterinarian on University Avenue. There, hating every moment of it, Rufus had his health checked out and was given some shots.

The next trip was across town to the office of the Humane Society, where Rufus was licensed. And then, still looking rather bemused over the whole thing, Parman took Rufus to his tobacco-smelling second-floor apartment and gave the dog an old blanket to sleep on.

Parman was a quiet man, who smoked, read, listened to good music on his stereo, and cooked nothing but hamburgers, because it was all he could cook. In the few days that followed Rufus lead a peaceful enough existence, but he didn't roam the campus anymore, even though the regents had left. Parman kept him on a leash when he went to his classes. And when he was in the lecture halls, he made sure that Rufus was outside the building, tied fast to something strong.

One morning, four days after he had gone to live with Dr. Parman, Rufus was tied by his new master to a steel fence post in the shade of a tree while Parman went to meet his morning class. Rufus lay quiet and content, full of dog food, until Parman came outside an hour later.

Parman wasn't alone. A tall man walked with him. Scenting the second man, Rufus lurched to his feet. He'd smelled this man before. That odor of lime aftershave mixed with the smell of *cats*. The hair on Rufus's spine rose as he growled at Dr. Burns.

Professor Burns stood over Rufus looking down while Rufus snarled, then the man said to Parman, "Do you know whose dog this is?"

"Mine, I guess," answered the young professor. "After all, a regent gave him to me."

Burns grunted. "It would take an act of the regents to get anyone to take him on. If you'd like, I'll tell you about his former owner. I even had custody of this animal for a time."

"*You* did?" Parman looked confused.

"I did, indeed, and not by choice. This dog lived under my house. But I am not the interesting one. Let me tell you about a student named David McCormick. You came here just this fall so you were spared knowing him. His nickname was Mad McCormick and he lived up to it."

As the two men went along together with Rufus jerking on his leash first to one side, then another, Dr. Burns recounted the tale of the skywriting, the bell tower climb, the green footprints up the library, and other pranks McCormick had been responsible for. He ended with the tale of the rubber chicken and the green smoke in the radio station.

"My word," said Parman at the end of the story. "And to think I missed all that. The bird landed in the lap of the governor." Suddenly he laughed. "I guess it was a joke on him."

Professor Burns laughed sharply. "He was only an innocent bystander. I suspect the chicken was meant to be a joke on me. In any event, let me tell you, I detest the very name of McCormick!"

"I can understand that. I have most of my problems with girl students, though. One of them at my last college told me that she was an expert in judo, and then she winked at me. She was one of the reasons I left and came here." Dr. Parman shuddered.

Rufus, who had stopped growling, sat down to scratch urgently at one ear. Dr. Parman had a heavy hand with the flea powder. As the dog scratched away, a cloud of yellow powder came out over Professor Burns's knees. The man moved away.

As he did, both men heard someone calling out to them at a distance. They looked ahead. So did Rufus, pausing with his left hind foot behind his ear, ready to scratch some more. He recognized the voice.

Down came the foot. He stood up.

A strange-looking couple were walking together down the concrete path that led to the bell tower from the dormitories. A short plump woman in a long white coat was waving her arms at the professors. The lanky red-haired boy walked in long strides beside her as she trotted to keep up with him.

"Rufus. Rufus!" cried Señora Perez.

"She knows him. Let the dog go," Professor Burns suggested to Parman.

Parman dropped the leash, and Rufus darted forward to greet his old friend. He licked Señora Perez's hands; then he looked up into the face of the red-headed, brown-eyed boy beside her. His nose was twitching as he scented the youth.

"Ah, Rufus, but I have missed you," said the woman. She took the setter's leash and waited for the two professors to come up. When they were there, she announced breathlessly, "Señores, this is Miguel Mc-Cormick. He is Davido's brother. The dog belongs to Miguel, because he belonged to Davido, who has gone away forever."

Parman had very quick wits for a man who dealt so much of the time with numbers, not words. He said to Miguel, "Fine. Keep the dog. He's yours. Are you a student here?" Parman was smiling with pleasure at the boy.

Professor Burns was not. To his way of thinking Miguel, or Michael, McCormick looked entirely too much like his brother. His voice was like his, too. He said, "Uh-huh, I got here last night. I know it's late to enroll, but I tried to drive my car here from Texas. I had to get her repaired six times, so it took a long time to make it to here."

Señora Perez said delightedly, "*Sí*, she did not make it all the way. She died in Phoenix!" How happy she had been to find another McCormick at the back door of her kitchen that morning. Davido had told Miguel where to find her and had told him, too, about Rufus and suggested that he ask Señora Perez to help him get the dog.

Miguel McCormick had been the "something" that was coming up. *Bueno*, now he was here.

"She's right," McCormick went on. "My car was an old clunker. She got as far as Phoenix, then she fell down and wouldn't get up, so I shot her and hitch-hiked here from there. I've got a scholarship."

"From the pecan growers?" asked Dr. Burns.

Michael turned a friendly freckled face toward the man. "Yeah, how did you guess? The scholarship sort of runs in our family."

"The family?" Burns wanted to know. "Are there more at home like you?"

"Yes, sir, there are. Three more of us. Two sisters and my little brother."

"That's a lot of McCormicks," said Professor Burns, as Señora Perez handed Rufus's leash over to Michael McCormick. As the boy patted the dog, making

friends with him, Professor Burns sighed and walked
off with Dr. Parman.

Señora Perez watched them go. Then as Michael
fondled Rufus's ears, she told him, "I will help you
feed him, Miguel, as I helped Davido. I am so pleased
that Davido is going to school in Texas."

"Oh, he'll get to be doctor yet," said Michael, as he
let Rufus off the leash. "That is if he doesn't get upset
and bust loose too often. You know what I mean."

As Rufus ran ahead of them toward a pair of Frisbee throwers, Señora Perez said in her deep sad voice,
"*Ay de mí*, I know what you are saying. What will you
study here, Miguel? Do you want to become a doctor
too?"

"Nope, not me. I want to study history. You know
—the kind where old kings chop the heads off their
wives when they get tired of them. The history of
England, most of all, I guess."

Señora Perez, who had started away, stopped in her
tracks watching Rufus jump for a descending Frisbee.
She put her hands to her cheeks, starting to worry
already. She'd noticed Professor Burns's face as he'd
left her and Miguel. It had turned to stone. She asked,
"Tell me, do you bust loose also?"

"Sure. All of us McCormicks do. It runs in the
family. You should see my mother. She throws frying
pans at Pa. Yes, I guess I do, too, when things get too
much for me."

Happy, she whispered "*Ay de mí*" again, as Rufus
bounded past her with the captured Frisbee in his
mouth and a Frisbee player chasing him.

ABOUT THE AUTHOR

Now a resident of Southern California, Patricia Beatty was born in Portland, Oregon. She was graduated from Reed College there, and then taught high-school English and history for four years. Later she held various positions as science and technical librarian. Recently she taught Writing Fiction for Children in the Extension Department of the University of California, Los Angeles. She has had a number of historical novels published by Morrow, several of them dealing with the American West in the 1860 to 1895 period.

Mrs. Beatty has lived in Coeur d'Alene, Idaho; London, England; and Wilmington, Delaware; as well as on the West Coast. Her husband, Dr. John Beatty, her co-author for a number of books, teaches the history of England at a major California university. One of their books, *The Royal Dirk*, was chosen as an Award book by the Southern California Council on Children's and Young People's Literature. The Beattys have a teen-age daughter, Ann Alexandra.